Her Sister

Her Sister

Search for Love Series

KAREN ROSE SMITH

For my husband, Steve, and my son, Ken,
who hold my heart.

Prologue

Where is Lynnie? Where did she go?

In her mind, five-year-old Clare Thaddeus called to her little sister—*Come back, Lynnie. Please come back.*

The huge policeman crouched down in front of Clare's mother at the sofa and said in a deep, slow voice, "Mrs. Thaddeus, I know you're terribly upset. But I need details. We've got an hour before daylight. If your daughter wandered outside—"

Clare's father, who'd been talking to another man in blue, glanced at her, and Clare huddled down deeper into the big green armchair. Her dad didn't come to her but rather went to her mom, sank down beside her and wrapped his arm around her. Then he spoke to the officer. "Our daughter, Lynnie, is three. She would never go outside into the dark on her own."

"Tell us again where you were last night," the policeman demanded in a not-so-nice voice.

"I worked late, preparing a brief."

"Until five a.m.?"

"Yes, until five a.m. As I told you, I always check the girls' rooms before turning in. Lynnie wasn't in her bed. I woke my wife. We looked through the whole house and then we called you."

Clare had been sleeping in her brand new room. They'd moved in here—she studied her hand and counted her fingers—five days ago. Boxes were still stacked down here and upstairs. The house was okay. There were more rooms for her and Lynnie to play hide and seek. But she didn't like being alone in her own room at night. She'd liked it better when she and Lynnie had slept in the same room.

Earlier she'd thought she'd heard Lynnie's door open...thought her sister was going to the bathroom and might come in and crawl into bed with her. But she'd been *so* sleepy. She and Lynnie had been running through the hose sprayer all afternoon in the backyard while Mommy unpacked. She was supposed to watch her sister. She was always supposed to look out for Lynnie. That's what big sisters did.

Where had Lynnie gone?

Then Clare remembered the blue car that had driven down the alley in back of the yard lots of times. The man had stopped once and watched them. But she'd thought he might be one of their new neighbors who just wanted to say hi.

Should she tell the policeman?

He was so big, and he looked mad. Her dad looked mad, too, as he asked, "Why do you want to question me and my wife separately?"

"That's just the way we do it, Mr. Thaddeus."

Although she was scared of the two big men in blue uniforms, she knew her mommy and daddy wouldn't let them hurt her. Policemen helped, didn't they? They were going to help find Lynnie.

She slipped off of the chair, went over to the sofa and tugged on her mother's arm. "Mommy, when I was playing—"

The doorbell rang.

"Are you expecting someone?" the policeman asked, his brows arched.

Not sounding at all like herself, her mother answered, "I called a friend."

"Before or after you called us?"

Her mother's face turned red. "*After*, of course."

"Mommy." She tugged on her mother's arm again while one of the policemen went to the door.

Her mother took Clare's hand. "Not now, honey. Natalie's going to take care of you for a little while so we can talk to the officers."

"But, Mommy—"

Her mom's best friend, Natalie Barlow, rushed into the living room looking as upset as her mom and dad. "What can I do?"

Her father answered quickly. "Can you take Clare upstairs? And can you call our old neighbors? Maybe they'll help search. I've got to get out there looking, but I have to finish answering questions first."

Natalie gave Clare a weak smile and took her hand. "Come on, honey. Let's go upstairs for a while."

Her mom kissed her.

Her dad gave her a nod.

She tried again. "When I was playing with Lynnie—"

Tears fell down her mom's cheeks. Her dad said, "Not now. Go upstairs with Natalie."

What she had to say wasn't important. The man in the blue car didn't matter. Only Lynnie mattered.

As Clare followed Natalie upstairs, she got very afraid. What if the policemen couldn't find Lynnie? Is that why her mommy was crying? Because she didn't think they could? Was that why her dad was mad?

Natalie bent down to her. "I don't want you to worry. Everything's going to be all right."

But Clare knew better. If Lynnie didn't come home, nothing would ever be right again.

Chapter One

"I'm not taking it back. I bought it with my own money." Shara Thaddeus stared at her mother defiantly, standing her ground. At sixteen, she was Clare's payback for the trouble Clare had given her parents when she was sixteen, though certainly not for the same reason.

At thirty-two and a single parent, Clare didn't know what to do with Shara any more than her parents had known what to do with her. She'd rebelled because she'd wanted their attention. *Any* of their attention. All of their attention. When Lynnie had been around, Clare had loved her and protected her and been her big sister. But after she'd disappeared, it was as if Clare hadn't existed. Everything was always about Lynnie. And Clare had just wanted her parents to realize that although her sister was gone, *she* was still there.

Shara, on the other hand, had always had all of Clare's attention. What she didn't have was a father. She'd been a precocious child, constantly testing her boundaries.

Sometimes Clare just got weary of being a watchdog. But yet wasn't that what parents were supposed to do?

After taking a deep breath for patience then putting her chin-length brown hair behind her ears, she reached out and took the blouse from Shara's hands. It really wasn't a blouse, just a stretch lace concoction that *her* daughter wasn't going to be caught dead in. "If you wear this out on the street, you'll get arrested. What did you buy to go with it?" She meant to keep her tone curious but it sounded judgmental anyway.

Shara produced a pair of black leather shorts that Clare suspected would fit too snugly.

"The outfit goes back. It's not appropriate for school. It's not appropriate to wear to the mall. It's not appropriate to be caught dusting the house in. What were you thinking?"

"I'm thinking there are a few boys who would think I'm hot."

Counting to ten had never been a strategy that worked well for Clare, especially when her daughter was deliberately trying to push her buttons. But she tried it again, nonetheless, not meeting with any more success than she'd achieved the last time. She prayed for patience, or wisdom or anything that would help deal with her daughter.

Finally, in a friendly tone she asked, "Care to give me their names? Maybe I can do background checks."

Shara studied her mother, trying to decide if she was joking or serious. "Brad said he likes me in black."

"Brad doesn't need to like you in anything. He's a senior. You're a sophomore. We've talked about this,

Shara. He has a reputation and I don't want him giving *you* a reputation."

"You are wound *so* tight," Shara mumbled.

Before Clare could deal with *that* assessment, the telephone rang. She glanced at it, thought about letting it ring, letting the answering machine take over. But maybe both she and her daughter needed a few minutes to cool down. She saw from the Caller ID that it was her mom's home number. This would probably be a short conversation. They never had much to say to each other.

Clare watched Shara take the new outfit and her other bags to her room. "They go back," Clare called after her.

Her daughter didn't bother to reply.

Clare greeted her mom with a chipper "hello," wondering what she was going to put together for supper. As an X-ray technician at the hospital, she usually arrived home after Shara. Today, however, Shara had asked her if she could stop at the mall for an hour or so after school and Clare had agreed. It looked as if they'd both be taking a trip after supper to return Shara's purchases. Maybe they should just leave now and grab pizza there. The mall on an October Friday night would be busy.

"Clare?"

The tiny crack in her mother's voice made Clare pull in a breath. "What's wrong? Has something happened to Dad?"

Although her father and mother had divorced two years after Lynnie had disappeared, Clare had desperately tried to hold onto bonds with both of them.

"I haven't heard from your father in weeks. The last

time I saw him was at the picnic you had Labor Day weekend."

It was really strange. Her parents had once had a good marriage until Lynnie was taken. Now they were awkward together whenever they had to be in the same room. Clare always felt as if she were the cause of that awkwardness, always felt as if she should do something to make it all better, always felt as if she was the neutral territory in the middle of a decades-old war.

After a short pause, her mother explained, "Detective Grove called me. He already spoke to your father."

Clare's heart skipped a beat. "Detective Grove?" The picture of a tall lean man in a rumpled suit flashed in her mind—the man who had taken over Lynnie's investigation after the patrol officers' first visit.

"Do you remember him?" her mother asked gently—too gently—and Clare had a shivery premonition of what could be coming.

"Didn't he retire?" she asked her mom, her heart racing now.

"Yes, he did. But he's not really keen on retirement and he's been...working a few cold cases." Her mother's voice was edgier than usual and a little wobbly, too.

"What are you trying to tell me, Mom?" Clare's hands became sweaty as she thought about all the possibilities. Lynnie's face at three and a half was still so vivid in her mind—the face they'd used on posters...the face she'd envisioned floating in a river...the face on the body in nightmares that had been buried in a ditch. The *not* knowing had always been worse than knowing. The not knowing is what had torn them all apart. Clare really believed that if the police had found Lynnie's body somewhere, maybe they could have gone on as a family.

Maybe.

"He wants to meet with us tomorrow morning. You, me and your dad. He thinks he has a lead."

Clare's throat went desert dry. Even though she'd only been five, she remembered the hope that had filled her parents' faces whenever a new lead had been phoned in, whenever the police had gotten a tip from an informer on the street, whenever there was a chance that Lynnie might have been spotted. She also remembered the expression on their faces when all those hopes had been dashed and one day had turned into the next without teaching them anything new.

Except that they were losing each other, hour by hour, day by day, week by week.

"What kind of lead?" Clare asked, trying to control the shakiness in her voice.

"He wouldn't tell me over the phone. He's working out of his home, so I offered the use of my office at *Yesteryear's Treasures*. Can you be there tomorrow at ten?"

Her father wouldn't like meeting at her mother's shop. Now and then he'd complained to Clare that her mother was lost in the past. He didn't like the mustiness of the store or what the old furniture represented—a history that couldn't be changed...a child who would never come home. Her mother didn't see it that way at all. Her mother liked to relive every memory she had. She wrapped herself in the reminiscence of what she told Clare were the happiest years of her life. More than that, *Yesteryear's Treasures* had given her a reason to get up each day, a reason to search for old furniture if not for her daughter, though Clare suspected she still looked for Lynnie everywhere she went.

Trying to prepare herself for the meeting, she shored up her courage and asked, "Did Detective Grove say whether this lead means Lynnie's alive or dead?"

A sharp intake of breath met her question and then her mom answered, "He didn't say, and I didn't ask. I still have hope, Clare. I always have."

Yes, her mother had held onto the hope that Lynnie was still alive, that some misguided woman had taken her and raised her for her own. But a misguided woman didn't steal a child from someone's house in the middle of the night.

False hope was worse than no hope at all. Clare and her dad understood each other on that one point, at least.

"I'll be there tomorrow, Mom, but please don't—" She wasn't sure how to say it.

"Please don't believe in the best rather than the worst? Oh, Clare. Maybe as you get older you'll learn that believing in the best is the only way to get through some days. I'll see you in the morning, honey."

Clare and her mother weren't on the same wavelength...would never be on the same wavelength. Just like her and Shara?

She said goodbye, hung up the phone and went to her daughter's room. Arguing with Shara would postpone thinking about the meeting tomorrow morning...a meeting that could shake up all of their lives once more.

Amanda Thaddeus stood before the 1930's hutch, staring through the glass door, barely noticing the ornate gridwork, hardly aware of the Belleek cup and saucer inside. Turning away from the hutch and the 1930's collection—the maple rocker, the oak desk, the European armoire—Amanda understood her search for antiques to fill her shop had been an ongoing quest to find Lynnie. Not that it made any sense. But she'd always looked everywhere, no matter where she went.

Couldn't her little girl be around that street corner? Hidden in a doorway? In the backseat of that car? She'd practically driven herself and Max crazy...until he'd spent less and less time with her...until they'd searched separately...until he'd started drinking.

Until he'd *stopped* drinking and found a cause.

Her cause had been a little different—to make a life for her and Clare without Lynnie, and then without Max. Oh, he was there for Clare when he wasn't working on an important case. He never shirked his financial responsibilities. But Amanda had found purpose in succeeding on her own.

The search for Lynnie had almost bankrupted them. Fortunately her own mother's legacy, a farmhouse filled with antiques, had given her the chance to make a living.

Yesteryear's Treasures mattered.

When the door to her shop opened and Detective Grove stepped inside, she felt almost dizzy with anticipation, both dreading and craving whatever news he'd brought. Her hands became clammy and that piece of toast in her stomach felt like it was jumping around.

Trying to hold onto her composure, she concentrated on the detective, seeing immediately the evidence of the passage of years around his eyes, his mouth, his thick jowls, his receding hairline.

"Detective Grove," she said in what she hoped was a composed, even tone.

"Mrs. Thaddeus." His gaze appraised her, probably noticing the difference the years had made in her, too, particularly her strawberry-blond hair. As a young mother she had worn it long. Now it framed her face in the natural waves she'd once despised with gray mixed into the strawberry blond. At fifty-six she'd come to terms with how her appearance had changed, how her body had changed and how her life had changed.

Before she could voice even one of her many questions, the ding of the bell sounded again and her ex-husband stepped over the threshold. She couldn't look at Max without remembering everything—the good, the bad and the ugly. Still, when she looked into those intense brown eyes—Clare's eyes and Lynnie's eyes— she couldn't quell a stirring deep inside of her that remembered intimacy with this man. His thick brows once as dark brown as his hair were laced with silver now. His angular face had an almost gaunt look this morning and she knew that was probably because he hadn't slept all night, just as she hadn't, thinking about what Detective Grove was going to tell them. In jeans, running shoes and a red windbreaker, Max looked less like the juvenile law attorney he was than a man ready for a weekend of whatever might come his way. But then, Max had always been prepared for anything.

Except for losing a daughter.

"Clare was pulling in as I came in." His deep voice resonated in the room.

No—*It's nice to see you, Amanda.* No—*How are you, Amanda?* No hug just to let her know he knew what she was feeling. But then she wasn't rushing toward him with an embrace, either.

The bell over the door tinkled again as Clare came into *Yesteryear's Treasures,* hugged Max and didn't let go for a long time.

Amanda could feel all of her daughter's anxiety, as well as her own. Clare didn't confide in her. That hadn't changed from when she was a teenager. But the deep down sadness and the fear that had been with Clare ever since Lynnie was taken from them, Amanda could feel, too. She'd been so lost in the search for Lynnie, in the absence of Lynnie, that she hadn't realized for a long time how deep that fear *was* in Clare—the fear that she'd not only lose her sister, but her mother and her father, too.

After Max released his daughter, Clare came to her. When Amanda put her arm around Clare's shoulders, her daughter stiffened and Amanda wished, as with so many other things, that this would be different, too.

"Do you want to do this in your office?" Detective Grove asked gruffly.

Leading the way, taking a deep breath of the past as well as potpourri, Amanda motioned to the open door at the back of the store. The space was small—a hutch with a computer, file cabinets, a set of bookshelves for all her reference books on antiques. Her swivel desk chair and the captain's chair always resided there, but she'd tugged in two ladder back chairs from the shop, so they'd all have someplace to sit.

"I'll be right back," she told everyone now. "I need to put the *Closed* sign on the door." She could have had one of her salesclerks come in today. But she hadn't wanted the distraction. She hadn't wanted chatter and laughter in the store. She hadn't wanted anyone else around after the detective left, no matter what he had to say. Composure was everything now, at least when others were around.

When she returned to her office, no one was speaking. Detective Grove sat with his hands clasped between his knees, staring at the floor. Max was watching Clare as she stared out the window. Clare and Lynnie had looked so much alike as children. If Lynnie was alive, would she and Clare look alike today? Probably not.

Amanda perched on her desk chair and waited.

Grove looked up, saw that she and Max were seated across the room from each other and didn't seem to know which one of them to address. Finally his gaze locked to Max's. "I know you want me to cut to the chase, so here it is. Luther Brown is on death row in Texas, awaiting execution for the murder of two little girls."

Amanda heard Clare's sharp intake of breath, saw her daughter wrap her arms around herself as if in protection for whatever came next.

"His sister," Grove went on, "was charged as a co-conspirator. But she made a deal, led the authorities to the bodies and got life without the possibility of parole.

It turns out she was diagnosed with cancer about four months ago—pancreatic cancer. It's moving fast and she doesn't have long to live. Apparently she held something back during the deal-making. No way to tell why. No way to tell whether loyalty to her brother was still important to her. But what she held back was a journal Brown had kept."

Amanda's heart pounded now and her gaze met Max's. Over the years, they'd learned more than they'd wanted to know about child abductions, kidnappings, pedophiles and anything else that might help them find their daughter. When Lynnie had been taken, there had been a minimal knowledge of all of it. Some police departments had been more well-informed than others. There hadn't been a Missing Children's Act or Amber Alerts then. Everything had been different. Everything had been disorganized. Everything had been a guess and a hope with little or no strategy and no organization.

From the research, she knew not all pedophiles were killers. But she also knew that in some pedophiles, their propensity for violence increased with each child they abused.

Tearing his gaze from hers, Max asked Grove bluntly, "Are you telling us Lynnie is dead?"

"No. That's not what I'm telling you. Hear me out before you jump to conclusions."

"Hear you out? Like you heard me out when Lynnie was abducted?"

Amanda could still hear the old anger ringing resoundingly in her husband's voice.

Only a day or so into the investigation, Grove's

suspicion had fallen on Max. But Max had passed a lie detector test. And once they had finally listened to Clare jabber about a blue car, everything had changed. Still, Grove had never apologized to Max for the hell he'd put him through.

Ignoring Max's question, Grove took a small notebook from his shirt pocket, flipped it open and studied his scribbles. "Brown's journal started in 1980. He's not an educated man but he *is* a smart one. He was trained as an electrician. My guess is he worked on your new house. He saw you when you came through with your family, checking it out from foundation to carpet laying. I suspect he was there the day the doorknobs were set. Either he stole a key or managed to rig the lock on that basement door that went outside."

"All the locks were the same," Amanda murmured, knowing one key unlocked them all.

"Convenient then and now. Some people still do that today who aren't security conscious. But in a little burg like Pine Hill, where no one even locked their doors back then, even just picking the lock wasn't a problem for somebody like him."

"Was Lynnie in his journal?" Clare's voice was small and she sounded more like a child than an adult.

"This is how it goes," Grove said with the lines around his mouth cutting a deep frown. "The journal had details, dates and places. When Brown first started doing this, the kids seemed to vary in age from three to seven. He snatched them, kept them somewhere for a while, then abandoned them."

Amanda knew there was a world of information

the detective wasn't giving them. But she didn't care right now. She just wanted to know what that journal said about Lynnie.

"Abandoned them where?" Max asked sharply.

"He drove them three to four hours away, left them at a church, or a school or a shopping center."

"What did he do with Lynnie?" Amanda couldn't keep the question inside.

"That's the thing, Mrs. Thaddeus. There was no Lynnie from Pennsylvania in his journal. But there was a Winnie, though. And another little girl, Barbara. He listed both of them as abandoned near Pittsburgh."

"Lynnie had a lisp and couldn't say L's," Clare told the detective. "They always came out as W's. She couldn't even get out Thaddeus most of the time. It came out as 'Saddees'."

Everything Clare remembered about Lynnie was right and apparently she hadn't forgotten even the smallest detail about her sister. Amanda watched the former detective assimilate Clare's information which might have been in the original report. After all these years, Amanda wasn't sure what the police still had on file.

"There are a couple of things I want you to keep in mind," Grove counseled them. "When Brown's sister told the authorities about the journal and they obtained a warrant and confiscated it, she also told them that her brother changed the little girls' names. During the time they were with him, he gave them a new name—a name from Louisa May Alcott's *Little Women*. So looking for Lynnie Thaddeus was a lost cause. What I did have were the Pittsburgh destinations and the possibility of four

names—Beth, Meg, Amy and Jo. I checked dates of foster children coming into the system from Pittsburgh and
surrounding locations. Although Brown's journal listed
both drop-offs as June, I could only find one child who
matched Lynnie's statistics—age, hair and eye color,
height. Her name is Amy. No surname was recorded until after her adoption. She was placed with a foster family
after she was abandoned at a shopping center. They
eventually adopted her. The FBI is involved and I have
legal roadblocks to deal with, sealed records, that kind of
thing. But I'm making progress and I wanted you to
know that. What I *don't* want to do is raise false hope.
This might not be Lynnie. A DNA test will be the only
way to find out. But it's something we've never had before. Something solid. And I thought you should know."

As Amanda glanced at Max, she saw the stunned
look on his face. This was something *he'd* never expected. *They'd* never expected. Not in a million years.
Clare looked...as if she were going to cry and Amanda
could feel her daughter's emotion in her own throat.

Unable to stay in her seat, Amanda went to her
daughter and knelt down beside her. "Are you okay?"

"I don't know. What if we go through all this and
this girl, this woman, isn't Lynnie? What if she's so
damaged—"

Max leaned forward in his chair. "Don't! Don't do
this until we know more. You could ask yourself a thousand questions and not have any of the answers."

"How am I supposed to *not* ask the questions,
Dad?" Clare's voice rose. "You didn't want me asking
questions back then, either."

"Because I couldn't answer them," he said evenly, "just as I can't answer them now." Max focused on Grove. "Is the FBI helping you or getting in your way?"

"Helping. That journal opened everything up again. And police departments aren't isolated like they once were. But there's a lot of dust that's collected in twenty-seven years and we've got to get that all brushed away before we can find the truth."

"Is there anything I can do legally to help push this along?" Max wanted to know.

"No. Nothing. I want you to stay out of it."

"This is my *daughter* we're talking about."

"Maybe. Maybe not. Light brown hair, brown eyes, height and weight that seem to match isn't a whole lot to go on. But put it together with the dates and circumstantially everything seems to fit. Bottom line is you know as well as I do that those puzzle pieces might not match."

Grove stood. "I'll let you know more when *I* know more."

Max's color was high. He speared his fingers through his hair and Amanda saw his frustration. She *felt* his frustration. But there was nothing she could do about it. Divorce changed everything. It had taken her too long to understand that. But she did now. She accepted it. It had taken her years to realize she could only change what was in her power to control.

"I'll see myself out," the detective said, obviously understanding their state of upheaval.

When Grove left her office, Max swore.

A tear ran down Clare's cheek.

As Amanda stood by Clare's chair and put her hand on her daughter's shoulder, she was filled with hope. She'd never believed Lynnie was dead, although reason, and Max and the world had told her over and over again to be realistic. Her reality had been different than everyone else's. Hope would be her life raft until they knew the truth.

Once they knew the truth, she wouldn't need a life raft...because she'd have Lynnie back home.

Chapter Two

"This is unusual. Since when do you sit in your backyard, alone at night, studying the stars?"

Startled, Clare's hand went to her chest until she recognized Joe Lansing's voice. She hadn't paid any attention to him for the first year he'd lived next to her in the West York neighborhood. Then she'd been forced to. One night he'd come to her door, his hazel eyes serious as he'd told her he was a member of the Army Reserve and he was being deployed again. His dad would be looking after his house on a regular basis, but Joe wondered if she'd keep an eye on it, too. A house standing alone for over a year at a time could use more than one watcher. He'd said it so easily and had been so laid back that she hadn't thought of refusing.

When Joe had returned from his stint in Afghanistan over six months ago, they'd discussed changes in the neighborhood. He'd told her he owed her for being his sentry and if she needed help with something, as simple as putting out the garbage, she should call him.

She hadn't, of course. Clare and men simply didn't mix. Well, maybe they mixed, but the result of the experiment was usually damaging. So she hadn't called him until Shara's makeup swatches had clogged up the toilet. That had been last summer. Since then, they discussed the weather whenever they saw each other, or Joe's dad's health. He'd had a hip replacement after Joe had returned from Afghanistan.

They weren't friends, yet they were friendly. She knew much more about him than he knew about her, although she sometimes saw questions in his eyes.

"Did you ever feel claustrophobic inside your own skin?" she asked him now as he loomed over her in the darkness. She didn't usually like men to loom over her. It brought back memories of uniformed officers the night Lynnie had been taken. But Joe— His looming seemed more...protective.

"Did you ever feel so restless that if you sat, you couldn't stay sitting? That if you walked, you couldn't walk far enough? If you breathed, you couldn't feel the bottom of your lungs?" Now where had all that come from? He'd think she was a nutcase.

He sank down beside her on the redwood bench that accompanied the picnic table on the patio. He was a good six inches taller than she was, lean and fit. So lean and fit she usually took a second look if he wasn't watching. He was a landscape architect and a partner with his dad in a nursery. She knew any muscles he had didn't come from a gym. They came from hefting trees, rotating bushes, pushing carts loaded with supplies.

"I felt that way after I came back from Afghanistan."

She remembered seeing the lights on in his house very late, night after night. They'd never talked about the time he'd been away.

But right now she was glad for any subject that would distract her from what was really on her mind. "Were you in Afghanistan the whole time?"

He rested his hands on the bench and looked up at the sky. "I was."

"Were you hurt at all?"

"I was lucky to come home with just a little bit of shrapnel under my skin. Some buddies weren't so fortunate."

She thought about a man risking the life he'd made for his country. "Can you be called up again?"

"Possibly. But I might be out of the Reserve in six months. I have to decide if I want to re-up."

"It has to be hard to have your life interrupted."

He shrugged. "Usually life is a series of interruptions."

As he studied her, tendrils of the porch light's yellow beams reached for them in the yard, but didn't quite touch them. They sat in shadows. She was glad about that right now. If he could see her face, too much would show. She wouldn't be able to talk to him as a neighbor on a fall night if she thought he'd guess what was going on inside of her. She shifted, wiped her palms on her jeans, tried to think about something other than the information Grove had given her.

"Is something wrong, Clare?" Joe's voice was quiet, interested if she wanted to talk, but nonchalant if she didn't.

She was ready to give her usual answer, the one that

would tell Joe nothing and keep a wall up between their lives. *I'm fine. I'm just tired. I have something on my mind, but I'll work it out.*

She made the mistake of turning toward him. There was concern on his face. Actual concern. She hadn't confided in anyone for longer than she could remember.

"Have you lived in York all of your life?" She thought he had, but she didn't know for sure.

"Except when I went to college."

"How old are you, Joe?"

His mouth twitched up at the corners. "I'm sure your questions are leading somewhere—" When she didn't come back with a jibe as she usually did, he replied, "I'm thirty-six."

He would have been nine when she was five. Too young, maybe...no way to know unless she asked. "Do you remember a child disappearing from Pine Hill a long time ago?" Pine Hill, a rural community, was located about five miles outside of York.

Joe looked blank for a moment. Then, as if old movies were playing in his mind, he murmured, "I remember conversation at dinner about a search for a little girl. My parents sat me down and gave me the lecture about not talking to strangers." His gaze searched her face. "Did that have something to do with you?"

"Lynnie was my sister. Someone took her from our house in the middle of the night. We brushed our teeth together. We said our prayers together. She gave me hugs and—" Clare rarely let emotion get the best of her. She'd already cried once today. She was *not* going to cry again.

"Clare."

He said her name so gently, so compassionately she had no choice but to stand up and head for the house.

But Joe was quick on his feet and clasped her arm. She shook him off. "I'm fine."

"Like hell."

She wrapped her arms around herself, trying to figure out how to end this conversation and make her exit.

"You've been dealing with this a long time and never gave a hint of it. What happened to bring it up now?"

He was perceptive. Too perceptive. Maybe that's why she hadn't revealed much of herself to him before. Joe wasn't like the guys she'd dated...avoided...rejected. She couldn't even put her finger on why. She just knew distance was better than closeness, simple neighborliness better than any type of familiarity.

Still, she'd started this and she had to end it. "It really doesn't matter."

"Yes, it does. Why can't you talk to me? It's not as if we're strangers."

"Aren't we?" Her question wasn't argumentative, just realistic. "What do you really know about me? What do I really know about you? We're neighbors. We're not friends."

His expression transformed from concerned to blankly neutral. His eyes, so gentle moments before, became unfathomable. His broad shoulders stiff now, he gave a slight shrug. "You know a lot more about me than I know about you. Ever since I moved in, I wondered why you kept to yourself. Why the weather report was our only conversation. Now I know. Apparently, you shut people out when your sister was abducted, and you still do."

"Don't make assumptions about me, Joe." The walls she'd constructed brick by brick shook a little. Her neighbor had that effect on her, and that's why she'd stayed away from him since his return.

Doing quick math he calculated, "You were eighteen when you had Shara."

"I was looking for love in all the wrong places," Clare quipped, wondering why he was bringing up her daughter.

"So her father wasn't your soulmate?"

If this was his way of fishing, she was going to cut the line. "There is no such thing."

The phone in her kitchen rang. Relieved and so grateful, no matter who was calling, she said, "I have to get that."

Joe made no comment as she hurried away from him. When she stepped inside her back door, her neighbor still stood by the bench.

Would he wait for her to come back outside?

He'd be waiting all night. She wouldn't return to their conversation again.

Yes, she shut people out...with really good reason.

She did not intend to get hurt.

No risk, no pain.

It was her motto to live by.

What was Brad Hansen's mo-ped doing leaning against the side of her house at one o'clock on a Monday afternoon? Clare asked herself as she parked in her carport.

She rarely missed work. Rarely took a sick day. Rarely asked for days off. But she'd arranged for someone to cover for her this afternoon because—

Because the impact of what Detective Grove had told them on Saturday was hitting her hard. Yesterday she'd been in a kind of shocked haze. Although she'd told Shara about the meeting, she couldn't talk to her daughter about Lynnie. It just hurt too much.

She'd hardly been at the hospital an hour this morning when the urge to delve into the old boxes in her closet with photos of Lynnie had been so strong that she'd decided just to take this afternoon to try and put the detective's news in perspective, maybe even brush off her bike and go riding until she was clear-headed again. Until she could push away the fear and anxiety of what they might find out about her sister.

However, when she saw that mo-ped, new concerns poured in.

She didn't slam her car door, just quietly closed it, then mounted the two steps to her kitchen door. She heard music pounding from inside. Music meant Shara was home. It meant she'd cut classes.

Trying not to jump to conclusions, considering the fact she might have forgotten a school holiday, teacher's meetings, early dismissal, Clare laid her purse on the counter and headed for the primitive thumping of the bass. The lyrics of some of the music Shara listened to made Clare's skin crawl. She could ban it from the house, but she couldn't control what her daughter listened to outside of the house...or when she wasn't here.

Clare's living room usually invited her into its comfort. When she'd finally managed to scrape together a down payment for a house of her own, a house Shara could grow up in, she'd had a very tight budget but lots of imagination and the intense desire to create a place that really felt like home. Although she'd bought secondhand furniture and made slipcovers from material bought at Wal-Mart, the dark blue and beige colors, the surplus of plants, the repainted and refinished wood furniture beckoned to Clare at the end of her work day.

The rancher had two bedrooms. Shara's was at the end of the hall. Her door was open, and music—Clare used that term loosely—blasted from inside.

Clare knew that for the rest of her life, as she pushed Shara's door open, the scene in front of her would be indelibly printed on her brain. Shara and Brad were naked. Her daughter's brown hair lay tousled across her pillow, while she looked up at a boy that Clare believed she didn't really know, her hands gripping his shoulders.

Rage propelled Clare forward first. She wanted to throw the kid off her daughter, knee him where it would hurt most, and shake him until he understood that Shara was too young to know what she was doing.

Reason told Clare that confrontation in anger never turned out well.

But how could she be reasonable when her daughter was having sex in front of her eyes?

Shaking, holding onto her temper with both hands, biting back words before they could spill out, she finally shouted, "Get off of her. Now!" Her voice seemed to get lost in the song lyrics, so she yelled louder. "Get off of her before I call the police."

The two kids on the bed froze. Their heads swung toward her.

Then in fast forward, Brad scrambled to the side of the bed.

Shara squeaked, "Mom! What are you doing home?" and pulled up the covers while Clare went to the iPod dock and switched it off.

Her insides churning, her head pounding although the music had stopped, she pointed a finger at Brad. "I could have you arrested for rape. You're eighteen. She's sixteen. Do you have any idea what you're doing?"

"She wanted it," he snapped defensively.

"Statutory rape," Clare declared, her voice rising. "My father's a lawyer. Do you think I don't know the law?"

Brad slid off the bed and reached for his jeans that were heaped on the floor. He didn't seem at all embarrassed and that made Clare even angrier. "This isn't the first time," he declared to Clare, looking her straight in the eye. "And it's up to Shara whether it's going to be the last."

Clare had felt powerless before. Having a stranger sneak into her house and steal her sister had taught her what violation felt like...what lack of control felt like...what uncertainty felt like. She'd tried so hard to make Shara feel secure, safe and protected. Staring at her daughter now, however, she knew Shara didn't want to be protected by her. And that hurt.

"Get out. I'll be calling your parents."

He shrugged into his shirt. "I only have a dad. He

lets me do what I want. What else can he do? I'm over eighteen." After he slipped on his boots, he looked at Shara. "My condolences, kid. Call me when you get out of jail."

When he exited the room, the smell of testosterone was strong. The silence that permeated the bedroom held everything in the world that Clare had ever said to Shara, everything in the future she might say. She knew if she didn't do this right she could lose her daughter. She didn't want the degrees of separation that she felt between her and her mother come between her and Shara, though she was afraid they'd already started piling up.

While she peered out the window and took a calming breath, she heard the vroom of Brad's bike start up. Why hadn't God sent a manual with every child born?

"So I'm grounded, I guess?" Shara asked with a look that was a tad too guileless, a tad too light.

"Will grounding do any good, Shara? Will handcuffing you to your desk, locking the door, barring the windows teach you anything about what you should be doing as a sixteen-year-old?"

"Mom..." Frustrated teenage impatience was evident in Shara's voice.

Well, Clare was just as frustrated. "You didn't just stay out past your curfew. You didn't just go to a movie that I thought you were too immature to see. You didn't just forget to hand in an assignment. You were having *sex*—an act that's supposed to happen between a man and a woman when they care about each other, when they're committed to each other, when they love each other and want to spend their life together."

"I guess that's what you believed when you had sex before you had me?"

The barb cut. "I was stupid, Shara. I was trying to get attention from a boy. And not just attention, but love, because I didn't feel my father loved me. Is that what you want to hear? If I thought telling you all about my mistakes would keep you from making them, I'd lay it all out. But you don't listen to me. And if you do listen, you don't hear what I say."

Shara's eyes had widened and she looked speechless for a moment.

Clare waved at the kitchen door. "That boy doesn't care about you. Oh, he might want to have sex with you again because it felt good. But three minutes after he's done, he couldn't care less about you."

"You're wrong."

"No, I'm not. But as I said, you're not going to hear what I'm saying. That's a sign of you not being adult enough to do what you were just doing. So, yes, you're grounded, until I can figure out how to make you grow up a little bit. You belong in school, learning what you need to learn so you'll have a future. Do you want me to call the school every hour to check if you're still there? Do you want me to take you to school and pick you up? Do you want me to come and sit in your classes beside you to make sure you pay attention, you learn and you study? Push me any farther, Shara, and that's exactly what I'll do."

Her daughter looked horrified at the thought, and Clare felt elated that she'd finally made a dent in her daughter's blasé attitude.

Shara got out of bed, plucked her robe from the

chair and slid it on. "You can't come sit beside me in school. You have to work."

"If I have to, I'll get my shift changed to evening. And I'll find a babysitter who can stay here with you to make sure you don't step out of this house."

With that threat hanging between them, Clare crossed to Shara's door, stepped into the hall and closed it behind her.

She was shaking all over.

Still, she went to the kitchen, pulled her address book from the drawer and found her gynecologist's number. She'd make an appointment for an examination for her daughter. Maybe the doctor could give her some guidance.

Along with a prescription for birth control pills?

Clare dialed the number, shut her eyes and wished she could talk to her mother about this. But she couldn't.

She'd just have to talk to a stranger instead.

Amanda's doorbell rang Monday evening. She looked around the kitchen in the apartment above her shop as if she were seeing it through someone else's eyes. It was ten p.m. and everything was out of the cupboards—all the spices, all the canned goods, all the packages of pasta, all the bags of beans.

She'd called Natalie and left a message. She'd known her friend would be out with the Red Hat Society tonight, but she'd had to talk to someone. Natalie would understand that when she heard the message.

Fully expecting to see her old friend, she stared through the peephole onto the stair's landing and almost jumped back. Max's face stared at her.

She'd actually thought about calling him yesterday and earlier tonight, but had rejected the idea both times it had popped into her head.

When she pulled open the door and he stepped inside, he didn't seem surprised by the condition of her kitchen. "I should have known you'd be reorganizing. You always do that when you're shook up."

"I'm relining the shelves."

"You're trying to take control of something you *can* control."

Max was six-foot and mostly silver-haired now...but thickly silver-haired. His hairline hadn't receded one little bit. His eyes were as dark brown as they'd ever been. Just looking at him—"

Just looking at him brought back too many memories. "Don't psychoanalyze me, Max. It won't do either of us any good." Crossing to the counter, she began to stack spices on the shelf she'd just lined.

"Have you heard from Clare?" he asked her.

She shook her head. "Have you?"

"No."

"She'll deal with this in her own way, just like she's dealt with everything else."

Amanda knew that wasn't right. She knew the three of them should be handling this together, should be holding onto each other, should be praying for the best. But when she and Max had fallen apart, Clare had been the casualty. Neither of them had realized it until she'd become an angry teenager—rebellious, defiant, and intent on getting her way any way she could.

"An FBI agent named Jacobs called me this morning. He told me basically the same thing Grove did. He said he wants to keep me informed. Did he call you?"

"Yes. This afternoon."

The silence stretched way too long between them, creating the awkwardness that was always there now. Max was dressed in black sweats tonight and she wondered if he'd been working out to control his stress level.

"Did you work today?" she asked, just to make conversation.

He raked his hand through his hair and unzipped his jacket, as if he intended to stay. "This morning. But I spent most of this afternoon on the phone. I called contacts to see what more they could find out about Luther Brown."

That would be just like Max, needing to be in the center of what was going on.

"I couldn't get any more than what Grove and Jacobs told us. If I thought driving to Pittsburgh or flying to Texas would do us any good—"

"You've got to let the authorities handle this."

"Like they did before? Maybe I could get those records unsealed faster. *I'm* the expert in juvenile law."

"Maybe Grove doesn't need an expert. Maybe he just needs a little time."

"Time? We've waited twenty-seven years!"

Her ex-husband's voice was sharp. At one time his tone would have hurt her. Now it didn't.

They stared at each other—long, hard moments as they remembered other words...other times.

"I shouldn't have come. I thought it would do us both some good, but I was wrong." He strode to the door.

"Max."

With his hand on the knob he turned to her. "What?"

"Why can't we just be people together? Why can't we just be parents together?"

"Because we still blame each other for losing Lynnie."

Before she could say, "But I *don't* blame you anymore," he was gone. Just like that.

Arranging the spices in alphabetical order just didn't have the allure it had fifteen minutes before.

Trying to ignore the mess, she went to the refrigerator, took out the carton of orange juice, found a stray glass on the counter and poured. Max had always stirred up more emotion than she ever wanted to feel.

Crossing to her living room, a feminine haven of cream roses, fern-green drapes, a pale pink and white Aubusson rug, she headed straight for the mahogany end table and opened the drawer. She removed a round tin with the picture of a saddle on the lid. Opening it, she took a whiff of the candle inside. Leather. Actually, it was more than the smell of leather. Mingled with it was a scent like old wood.

She'd found the candle on a buying trip last winter. It had been tucked into the corner of a hutch in a little shop that had sold secondhand items. As soon as she'd uncapped it, the scent had taken her back to a time and place where happiness was still a butterfly that could land on her shoulder.

Sinking down onto the sofa she took another whiff, and there she was, eighteen, helping her dad with the summer crop of tobacco. She'd lived on a farm in Pine Hill with her parents. Her dad had raised tobacco for many years, along with corn and hay. He'd also raised turkeys, and every Christmas opened his fields for anyone who needed a Christmas tree. Farming had been tough even back then.

The summer after her senior year in high school she'd been helping her mom make sticky buns when Max had come into the kitchen with her father. She'd recognized him, of course. They'd taken an advanced geometry class together. Physics, too. There were lots of stories buzzing about Max, but she didn't know which ones were true and which weren't. She'd heard his mother had died in childbirth. She'd heard his mother had left when he was just a little boy. She'd heard his dad drank a lot and couldn't hold a job. That day she hadn't cared what she'd heard.

When her gaze locked to his, the sensation she experienced was as if the hot, gooey syrup from the sticky buns was running through her, making her feel all melty and weak.

Her father, a short balding man who was getting heftier each year, gave his wife and daughter a grin. "Just wanted to introduce you to my new help. Max Thaddeus, meet my wife, Mrs. Fogelsmith and my daughter, Amanda. Do you two know each other from school?"

"Yes, sir," Max answered without hesitation. "Amanda and I had a couple of classes together."

"Well, good, because you two will be working side by side some of the summer. Amanda helps with everything around here, including spearing the tobacco leaves on the laths. I don't let her have anything to do with hanging them up to dry, but she works beside me whenever she can."

Amanda felt like an idiot, standing there staring at Max, as if she didn't have a brain in her head. "Are you going to be working here today?" she asked, then realized maybe she shouldn't have. Maybe she shouldn't have sounded as if she'd be glad if he was.

"If I do a good job this morning, your dad might keep me on for the afternoon."

George Fogelsmith chuckled. "Ain't that the truth? You come with good references, boy. I don't think we'll have a problem. First I'll show you around the barn, then we'll head for the turkey pen."

Quickly, Amanda tore off a large piece of aluminum wrap, slipped three of the already baked sticky buns onto it and folded up each end until she had a small package. Then she crossed to Max and held it out to him. "For your lunch break."

George planted his hands on his hips. "Don't I get any?"

Amanda felt her cheeks go red. "Sure you do, Dad. I'll wrap yours up separately." She did that quickly and gave her dad a small package, too.

He winked at her and suggested, "Come find us when you're done helping your mom with the buns.

You can teach Max the fine points of mucking out stalls." Her dad's eyes twinkled at her and she knew *he* knew she'd be glad just to be around Max.

If her dad got busy and they'd have to do chores alone, maybe she'd find out which rumors were true about Max and which weren't.

The phone rang.

Amanda came crashing back to the present. Returning to the kitchen, still holding the candle in her hand, she picked up the receiver.

"Amanda, it's Max."

She closed her eyes and saw the boy he used to be...the girl she used to be. "I wish you hadn't left so...abruptly."

He didn't reply right away, but then he said, "I'm flying to Dallas as soon as I can arrange it."

"Does Detective Grove know?"

"No. I'm going to see what I can find out."

"Max."

"Don't worry, Amanda. I'll be discreet. I have to do all that I can to get to the truth, sooner rather than later."

"Good luck," she whispered, her voice catching. Old memories always did that to her...made her wish for a time she could never have back again.

When Max said "goodbye," she closed the lid on the candle.

"Finally," Shara muttered as she sat at her computer late Monday night. A reply to her e-mail had finally come in. She read it greedily, so grateful she had this one friend she could count on.

Shara—I'm so sorry to hear about what happened. You must have been so embarrassed, not only by your mother, but by your boyfriend. If he's still your boyfriend. You told me that you love him, but do you? Do you really? Can you love someone who's so cavalier about you and your feelings and what's good for you?

Shara had no idea what "cavalier" meant. She could look it up on the dictionary app. But it didn't really matter. She read on...

I know you're a beautiful girl. Anyone seeing your pictures on Branches knows that. If Brad can't see your beauty then he doesn't deserve you.

If you were here with me, I'd take you for a cable car ride to the top of Sandia Peak. You could look down onto the whole world and maybe put it all in perspective. Since you can't be here, I'll put a couple of pictures up on my page and you can take a virtual trip.

Why don't you come to the chat room and have a little fun? We'll talk about everything that doesn't matter.

Justin

Justin was so different from Brad. She could tell him anything. She could tell him everything. He seemed to understand it all, from cutting classes to wanting to wear trendy clothes, to hating how her mother kept tabs on her. His profile said he was a year older than Brad. Nineteen.

She typed in, *Let's go to the chat room,* and hit SEND. At least *there* she could be herself. At least *there*, her mother couldn't tell her what to say, do or feel.

Chapter Three

"Yes, I'm Mark Hansen, but if you're selling something—"

Clare squared her shoulders, ready to take on Brad's father Wednesday evening. She'd been leaving phone messages for him for two days and he hadn't bothered to answer them. She hadn't gone into detail, not wanting to put him on the defensive.

Now, he'd finally picked up his phone and she was going to make sure he knew what had happened. "I'm not selling anything. Your son is dating my daughter."

The silence that followed was rife with all the questions he wasn't asking. He finally settled on, "Is there a problem?"

"Yes, there is. Your son is eighteen. Correct?"

"Yes, he is." Hansen sounded wary.

"My daughter, Shara, is sixteen. When I came home early on Monday, she'd cut classes and they were having sex in her bedroom. I walked in on them."

"Maybe you should have knocked," he wisecracked.

Clare counted to fifteen. She knew people often said strange things when they were surprised or upset. She didn't know which Mr. Hansen was. She didn't care. All she cared about was protecting her daughter—the daughter who still wasn't speaking to her.

"As I said, Mr. Hansen, your son's eighteen, my daughter's sixteen. What he was doing to her was grounds for statutory rape."

"Hey! Wait a minute. They're two teenagers having some fun."

"Unprotected fun." Unfortunately she hadn't been able to get Shara an appointment with her gynecologist for another two weeks.

"What was your name again? I didn't catch it on the machine."

"My name is Clare Thaddeus. Your son isn't a good influence on Shara and I'd like you to talk to him."

"You work at the hospital, don't you? Brad pointed you out to me last month. He'd had an accident on his bike and needed X-rays."

"I don't remember seeing him there—"

"Oh, you didn't take care of him. You came running through looking for a patient."

She didn't know what any of this had to do with anything. Certainly not Shara. "Mr. Hansen—"

He interrupted her again. "Call me Mark."

"All right. Mark. Do you think you could have a talk with Brad? I really believe he's too old for her. At the least, he needs to respect the rules she lives under. I don't want her cutting classes to be with him." She didn't want Shara spending time with Brad Hansen at all, but she couldn't just come right out and say that, could she?

"I think we should talk about this. Are you busy this weekend? We could catch a bite to eat somewhere."

Her hesitation was obvious.

"Look, Clare, Brad's not a bad kid and I'm sure your daughter isn't, either."

"Of course, she's not!"

"Right. Well, maybe we could give each other a little support. Think about meeting me somewhere this weekend. You have my number."

"Will you talk to Brad? "

"We had the birds and bees talk a long time ago," he said tersely. "What else would you like me to tell him?"

"Tell him Shara is off limits."

She hung up. Her instincts told her speaking to Mark Hansen longer or meeting him somewhere would serve no earthly purpose.

"Soda water do it for you?" Frank Grey, a law school buddy of Max's from Dickinson, slipped onto the stool next to him at a Tex-Mex bar in Dallas, Texas, Thursday at lunchtime.

"Soda water has to do it," Max said agreeably, greeting his old friend.

"Then why did you want to meet here? We could have picked any restaurant."

"I hear the chili verde and the tortillas are the best

in the state. Besides, every once in a while I have to remind myself how stupid I was twenty-whatever years ago. It helps to keep me on track now."

He extended his hand to Frank and they shook. "You look good." Max hadn't seen Frank for five years. "I think more hair dropped from the top of your head to your face, though."

Frank's beard had grown fuller and a little longer as the hair on top of his head had thinned. But in a tan suit and a brown-striped tie, his cream shirt not having lost all its starch, he was a pretty good specimen after having lived over half a century.

Frank shrugged. "Ellie seems to like it. After thirty years, I still try to keep her happy." Shifting on the stool, he faced Max more squarely. "You said on the phone you got to town on Tuesday. You also sounded frustrated. What can I do?"

Frank's corporate law practice had nothing to do with the kinds of cases Max now tackled in the arena of juvenile law. But Max often tapped into lawyer friends across the country when he was testifying before Congress, helping representatives write new legislation, keeping tabs on the child abduction network and organizations for missing children. Frank had donated generously to a couple of Max's causes and helped him with contacts in Texas.

"I don't think there's anything you can do." Max had filled in Frank on the phone with everything Grove and the FBI had told him. "Just keep your ear to the network. I know you hear things. When I met with the FBI here yesterday, the agent was understanding and empathetic. But he didn't have new information. Apparently their office in Pittsburgh has been working closely with Grove. He found all this but they're putting their resources behind him. I thought since Brown's journal was unearthed in Texas, I could find out other details here. But either no one knows any more or they're just not telling because it's an ongoing investigation. You know how that goes. I even had an appointment with the Dallas D.A. yesterday, but he's as closemouthed as the rest of them."

"Their secrecy might have more to do with the families of the girls listed in Brown's book than with Brown himself. After all, he's on death row. What more can they do to him except execute him?"

"Yeah. What more can they do to him?" Max knew his fury and bitterness were in his voice, but there was nothing he could do about that. Both had settled in his gut and become old friends.

"Is the soda water really going to get you through this?" Frank's steady brown eyes wanted to know the truth.

"You mean waiting to find out whether my daughter's dead or alive?"

"That and dredging it all up again."

By *all*, Max knew exactly what Frank meant. Besides the abduction, there had been the disintegration of his life—the disintegration of his marriage and his family as he'd known it. He'd been powerless to stop it. He didn't cope well with being powerless. Never had, never would. That's why he'd come to Dallas while Amanda sat in her antique shop waiting for the call she hoped would come. Those were the kind of differences that had torn them apart. She'd chosen antiques. He'd chosen child advocacy.

"How's Amanda?" Frank asked quietly as if he'd read Max's thought process.

At that moment the bartender strolled up the bar from the group he'd been serving at the other end and nodded to Frank. Frank glanced at Max with an unspoken question—*If he ordered liquor, would it bother his friend?*

"Order whatever you want," Max insisted. Not long after he'd joined AA, he'd learned how to be around booze and other people drinking it. It was never a cakewalk, but he'd become detached from it. He'd just made everything else in his life matter more.

Frank opted for the easy way out. "Just give me whatever's on tap."

The bartender, with a spring of youth in his step, gave him a thumbs up sign and went to fetch the beer.

Frank's gaze met Max's and Max knew he'd have to answer his friend's question about his ex-wife. "Amanda and I don't talk much. She's all emotion right now. I can't deal with that."

"She's not the one who fell apart when Lynnie was abducted."

"I didn't fall apart," Max snapped. "I just reached for a different kind of comfort than she did."

The truth was, his wife had wanted to reach for him when he'd been unavailable, wrapped up in searching, neck-deep in fear and panic. She'd turned to her friend, Natalie, and anyone else who could sympathize.

He'd turned to no one. When it had been clear they weren't going to find Lynnie or her abductor, he'd drowned himself, not only in the alcohol, but in the fury...in the anger...in the regret.

"If I know Amanda..." Max said with a shake of his head. "...she's filling her head with dreams about a happy reunion. Even if Grove and the FBI find Lynnie, I doubt if there's going to be a happy outcome. If that had been possible, Lynnie would have found her way back to us. Since she didn't, I don't even want to think about what that monster did to her."

His hand was tight around his glass. The whiteness of his knuckles made an impact, and he released his grip. It wasn't as if he didn't know what happened to children who were abused. He dealt with it all the time. And the results weren't pretty. They were affected for the rest of their lives. Cases didn't have to be extreme for that to happen. And in Lynnie's case... He closed his eyes but that didn't erase the images that had burned a place for themselves in his nightmares.

"I wouldn't want to be you," Frank muttered sincerely.

The bartender slid his mug in front of him and the foam sloshed onto the bar. "If we could go back to Dickinson and do it all again—"

It was strange, but thinking about his law-school years at Dickinson didn't evoke scrapbook pictures of study-groups and campus life but rather memories of Amanda—how she'd worked beside him...waited up for him...kept a tight budget with him...loved him. And thinking about those years took him back further to a place he hadn't been in a long time—her dad's farm.

The coiled tension inside his chest released just a little. Those summer days on the farm.

He'd been working at the Fogelsmith farm for a month, staying away from Amanda, telling himself he had a career and a future to tend to. Everyone knew law school, like med school, didn't bode well for any kind of relationship. He'd been looking forward to college, dating lots of girls, not just one, adding notches to his belt, which if he had to admit it, wasn't very notched at eighteen. With studies, sports, scholarships in his sights and working part time, who had time for women? Or getting laid?

Amanda had been different from most of the girls who usually turned his head, or at least got his hormones revved up. For one thing she'd been skinny, with not many curves. For another, he'd never particularly liked redheads. Not that he'd made a study of it. But girls he'd taken to the homecoming dance, Christmas bash, or the odd party had been brunettes. Amanda had been in a few of his classes and she was quite intelligent. In class she was the one who knew all the answers when a teacher called on her. She obviously studied hard. Yet he never saw her around much before and after school. He realized why once he'd started working on her dad's farm.

Amanda's chores took up her out-of-school spare time. She loved animals, especially the kittens in the barn. And she helped her mom cook, too. That's why he never saw her in the library in the morning comparing her homework with her other classmates. That's why she didn't attend sports events. Amanda had always been her own person. As long as she was doing what she thought was right, nothing else mattered. He'd liked that about her back then. Now it usually annoyed him.

No other girl he'd known had ridden on a flatbed wagon in back of a tractor helping her dad or walked through the three-foot high tobacco field with him and her father, topping off the leaves, breaking off the flowers, pulling the suckers to make the leaves larger, thicker and darker.

There had been something almost intimate between them while they'd walked through the tobacco plants, their fingers reaching for the same flower now and then, their eyes locking, the sun beating down on them. Amanda had tied her hair back with a blue paisley handkerchief. It was obvious her fair skin sunburned easily, and she'd told him her mother made her put some kind of cream on before she went out. He could still remember the sweet smell of it, along with the tobacco, sunburned weeds, the scent of dried earth.

They'd come in from the field late that July afternoon. While he'd gone to the barn to help with the animals, Amanda had run toward the house, her scarf torn free, her red hair fiery in the afternoon sun. And he'd just stood there, a kid with a hard on, knowing Amanda Fogelsmith sent a shiver through his body that wouldn't quit, even in ninety-five degree heat. He slipped back in time to that night with no reluctance at all.

It was almost 6 p.m. when Amanda came around the corner at the barn and caught him washing off the day's grime and sweat at the water spigot. The temperature hadn't dropped a degree. The barn had been stifling and he'd just needed to let the cold water cool him down before he went home to stuffy rooms, cigarette smoke and the vacant sense of despair that always hung there.

He heard the soft "oh," before he saw her, lifting his head from the spigot, not attempting to wipe away the water dripping down his face. She was a dream that was too good to be true in a white peasant blouse with flowers embroidered on the front and jeans that showed off her long legs. Her hair looked loose and soft and flyaway, like she'd just washed it, and he could smell the scent of something like orange blossoms. She always smelled so sweet.

She made a point of keeping her eyes on his. "Mama said you're welcome to stay for supper. It was a long day."

He swept his hand over his face and felt like an idiot, dripping in front of her. "I'm not fit company." He motioned to the T-shirt he'd balled and thrown on the ground next to the spigot.

Her gaze wavered then, dropped to his chest, came back up to his eyes. "My dad probably has a shirt he can lend you. That is if you want to stay. Meatloaf with mashed potatoes and green beans, if you're wondering. I think Mama baked a cherry pie, too."

He almost laughed. If her company wasn't enough, she was trying to entice him with her mother's food because she wanted him to stay. He could see that, as plainly as he knew he shouldn't.

He couldn't keep the huskiness from his voice as he asked, "And what happens if I stay, Amanda?"

She pretended she didn't know what he meant and shrugged. "You get a great meal. My parents said—" She stopped.

"Your parents said I probably wouldn't get one at home?"

"No, I didn't mean—"

"Yes, you did. Yes, *they* did. And they're right. My dad's drunk most of the time and doesn't care whether we eat or not."

He took a few steps closer to her, not sure whether he wanted to intimidate her or make temptation escalate so he couldn't resist it. "You didn't answer my question. What happens if I stay?" He brushed her hair behind her ear and it was just as soft as he imagined it would be.

"I don't know," she managed breathlessly.

He was breathless, too, just looking at her, definitely from touching her. "I don't need a steady girl. I have plans."

Her shoulders squared and her chin came up. "I have plans, too. I want to be a teacher. I think you're awfully full of yourself to think I'd want you as a steady."

His grin was slow in coming, but it came, as he wrapped his arm around her and pulled that pristine peasant blouse right up against his chest. "Let's just see if we should even consider steady or not."

There had been no finesse in that first kiss. It had been filled with raw, teenage hunger. In short of a minute her hands had been on him, his hands had found her bottom in her jeans and the world had turned into a different place when they were done.

That had been the beginning of him and Amanda. So very different from the end.

When Frank thumped his empty beer mug down

onto the bar, he broke Max's fall into the past. "How about some of that chili you mentioned. I'm ready to burn a hole in my gut. How about you?"

Max wondered if the spicy food could possibly exacerbate the acid that had started burning there from the moment he'd gotten Grove's phone call. "Chili sounds good. That and the cornbread should hold me until I get home. I sure won't get any food on the plane."

"What time do you leave?"

"I'm flying out at five. I just wish I had something to take back with me...something more than the knowledge that Lynnie was one of Luther Brown's victims and there are probably too many more to count."

"You've got to hang onto the hope that she's still alive."

Max *was* hanging onto that hope. But even if Lynnie was still alive, that didn't mean he'd get his daughter back.

That was the worst fear of all—that his daughter could be so changed he'd see nothing but distance in her eyes.

Shara lifted her bedroom window Friday afternoon and heard the SUV next door start up in the driveway. Damn. That meant their neighbor had been home. Had he seen her sneak into the house? His carport faced their carport.

What were the chances? One in a million. Her mother would never know she cut classes again. She was getting really good at lying, making up stories that were close to the truth so she didn't screw up.

The October breeze still carried the hint of summer as it puffed the blue-and-white striped curtains away from the window. Shara looked around her room that her mother had decorated for her. They'd bought along the curtains from the small apartment where they used to live. Why was it her mother still treated her like she was ten. So did her grandparents, for that matter.

All the adults in her life were preoccupied with her missing aunt. Her mom never talked about her. There were pictures of Aunt Lynnie as a little girl at Gram's place. If they found her now—

That would be just too weird!

Shara thought about going to the refrigerator for something to eat. But she just wasn't hungry, hadn't been for about a week, which was fine with her. It wouldn't hurt her to lose a few pounds.

Picking up the phone on her nightstand, she sank down onto her bed. She'd been trying to call or see Brad ever since her mom had ordered him out Monday. But he wasn't returning her calls and she kept missing him at school. She'd gone over to his house before she'd come home. She'd had to take a bus and that had taken forever. But he hadn't been there.

So now all she could do was try to call again. Her mouth went dry so she took a few swigs of a bottle of water that she always carried with her. She'd walked from his house home and that had been about a half a mile. The bottom of her feet burned in her sneakers. She didn't want him to believe she was chasing him, yet she loved him, didn't she? Didn't he love her? He'd had sex with her. He'd liked it. He couldn't do that without feeling a lot for her, could he?

This time when she dialed, he answered!

"Hey, Shara." He'd obviously seen her number on his Caller ID.

She wished her mom would buy her a cell phone, but these days her mom wouldn't be doing her any favors. "Hey, Brad. I haven't seen you around or heard from you for a while."

"I took a few mental health days. You at school?"

"Are you kidding? No, I'm home. Do you want to go somewhere?"

"Can't."

When he didn't explain, Shara waited. The silence lengthened. "Maybe we could do something tonight," she suggested.

"Sorry, I've got stuff to do. And, hey, somebody's beeping me. I've gotta go. Talk to you later."

The dial tone sounded in her ear.

Had her mother spooked him? Did he really think her mother would press charges against him? Shara swore, tossed the cordless phone down onto the bed and went to her computer desk.

She leaned down to the cubbyhole on the lower right to turn on the tower. But as she started to straighten, a wave of dizziness rushed over her and she steadied her world by clutching the desk.

Damn. What was going on? She was never sick. No appetite...tired...dizzy. The flu?

Or...

Her period was a week late. Suddenly it all came together. Panicked, she grabbed for her purse. She had to get to a drug store.

And if the pregnancy test was positive?

She ran down the hall and out of the house, too scared to even think about the answer.

Chapter Four

The motorcycle zoomed up the street with enough destructive noise to wake every zombie on the planet. Clare was sure the house shook as it pulled into her driveway and she glanced out the window. The figure on the bike wore a black helmet.

Clare had just gotten home, checked on Shara who was still not talking to her and had begun to stir together a meatloaf. Now she stopped when there was a pounding on her kitchen door.

"Just a minute," she called, washing, and soaping, and washing her hands again. She carried the towel with her as she went to the door.

When she opened it, the man said, "Mark Hansen. You must be Clare."

Brad's father was all good-looking charm, mussed hair, motorcycle helmet under his arm. She wasn't sure if she should let him inside the house or not, so she stood where she was. As far as she was concerned, he'd been rude, as rude could be.

It seemed that he knew that. He gave her a boyish smile. "I thought I'd come over in person to apologize."

She didn't know if she wanted Shara to hear this conversation, so she told him that. "My daughter's home and I don't want her to overhear. Do you mind if we talk in the carport?"

"Not at all." He stood down the two steps and waited for her to do the same.

His gaze canvassed her, from bangs to espadrilles. This was a man who was used to women falling at his feet. She could tell.

"I didn't mean to be so flip on the phone," he said, his smile still lingering. "I talked to Brad and hopefully convinced him that young love isn't what it cracked up to be. I warned him that Shara is definitely too young for him to be involved with her."

Was that why Shara was holed up in her room? Because Brad broke up with her? Clare wished her daughter would talk to her, really talk.

"Did Brad agree with you?"

"Let's just say a little bribery doesn't hurt. I convinced him I'd pay to get his bike overhauled."

"And that's all it took?"

"You must know how young men think, Clare. What he thinks he wants today, he won't want tomorrow. Boys his age want immediate gratification. But I pointed out that sometimes that gratification will get him into very hot water."

This is what Clare wanted, of course. On the other hand, she'd hoped Shara had chosen a boy who would really care about her. If Brad would give her up so easily, then he really was a teen-age jerk.

"Do you believe Brad when he tells you he'll stop seeing her?"

"Sure."

She tilted her head and studied him. "You don't think he's telling you what you want to hear, so he can do what he wants."

"Boy, you are suspicious."

"I'm cautious."

"Brad and I look out for each other. When his mom left, we knew we had to count on each other."

How she wished she and Shara could count on each other. Shara could count on her. She just didn't realize it. "I'm glad we could settle this. Shara's going to be hurt, but a little bit of hurt now is better than a lot of hurt later."

"You're right about that," he agreed.

Clare thought he'd turn and go, but he didn't. His gaze ran over her again until he asked, "How would you like to go out this weekend? I know a great club—"

"No."

He blinked as if he never expected that. "No? Just like that? Without even thinking about it?"

"First of all, I don't date. I have too much on my plate. And second of all, Shara would think I was knifing her in the back if I went out with you."

"You wouldn't have to tell her."

"I don't keep secrets from my daughter."

"Brad was right, you are as straight as they come. No fun at all. Maybe that's why your daughter has turned to her wild side."

And with that, Mark Hansen turned, hopped on his bike, started it up, and vroomed out of her driveway. She watched as he rode down the street, hardly stopped at the stop sign, then took a right.

This was exactly what she'd wanted, wasn't it? Then why had the whole conversation made her feel empty inside? The night air was turning cooler and she rubbed her arms, a chill running up her back. Maybe she was over-reacting to everything.

"Clare."

When she heard Joe call her name, she over-reacted to that, too. Why, after all this time with him as her neighbor, she was suddenly more nervous around him, she didn't know. Maybe because she'd told him something personal, something she didn't talk about with anyone, not even her parents. Especially not with her parents.

The idea that Lynnie could be alive—

She was glad Joe came to the back entrance of her carport just then, glad she had something to distract her.

"Hey," she said with a smile. "You're home early."

He gave her a wry grimace. "Some days I do get home in time for dinner at my own house instead of buying take-out."

"You work a lot."

"Yeah, I do, but that's because there's nothing waiting for me at home."

She couldn't tell exactly how he meant the statement, but it seemed to be an opening line to something else, some insight about him, some yearning he still had.

Now she was really over thinking. "Did the motor-cycle bother you?"

"Not since he left."

She laughed. "That was the dad of the boy Shara was dating."

"*Was?*"

"Hopefully *was*. He said he talked with Brad and made him realize he's too old for Shara. But if he broke up with her, I'll have to contend with that."

"I wanted to talk to you about Shara."

"I don't understand." Did he want to give her advice on how to raise her teen-age daughter? She needed it, but she waited, not wanting to jump to any conclusions.

"I didn't just get home early today. I worked at home all day catching up on bookkeeping. So before I accuse Shara of something she didn't do—Did she have the day off school? The afternoon off? Something like that?"

"No."

"Then she cut classes because she was here this afternoon. I was in the kitchen around one and I saw her going into the house."

Cutting class again. More to add to the grounding list. "I don't know what to do with her."

"She won't talk?"

Clare just rolled her eyes.

"She probably learned that from you, the eye-rolling, I mean."

She realized he was probably right. "Thanks for telling me about her being here today. I'm going to have to tell her you saw her. Will that be a problem?"

"Not for me. She'll probably call me a tattle-tale, but I've been called worse."

Again Clare had to smile in spite of everything. She liked Joe's sense of humor. She liked the way he put things in perspective. She certainly needed that right now.

"I'd better go in and put the meatloaf in the oven. Then she and I have to talk. I'd invite you to supper, but–"

"Yeah, I have a feeling that's not some place I'd like to be tonight."

"I'd rather skip it myself."

Unexpectedly he laid his hand on her shoulder. "Don't be too hard on yourself. Being a parent is the toughest job in the world, I hear."

The touch of his hand on her shoulder created sensations in her she hadn't felt in a very long time. There was heat and a bit of excitement and a deep-down longing that once belonged to a dream.

But she didn't know if she wanted to dream again and she would have backed away, but she didn't have to because he dropped his hand. "Take care, and if you need to call in the troops, I'm only a phone call away."

When he loped back to his house, it was hard for Clare to tear her eyes from him. She did, though, because she had more than one responsibility that prohibited dreams.

Teenagers on lunch break roamed the campus on Monday as Shara stood in the shade of the bleachers with

Brad. He was looking everywhere but at her and that scared her. Why couldn't he look her in the eye? Why was he constantly checking his watch? Why couldn't he be like Justin? She'd e-mailed him a lot over the weekend. He was always there for her and seemed to understand everything she was feeling.

Maybe Brad would too, once he knew.

"I know my mom probably scared you."

"Nobody scared me," he protested, still looking down at his sneakers.

"I have some news that could change everything."

Now he did give her a glance. "What kind of news? Did you win the lottery or something?"

She supposed money could change her life, but not as much as this. "I'm pregnant."

Now he stared at her but he didn't speak. His jaw had dropped open a little. He looked as if there had been an earthquake and he was barely left standing. Welcome to the club. She knew what that felt like.

He let out a string of curse words her mother would be totally unhappy with. She didn't like them much herself. She grabbed his arm. "Brad, this is serious. We have to figure out what we're going to do."

He went rigid and now his stare almost hurt her in its intensity. "*We're* not going to do anything. I have nothing to do with this. It's on you. You should have been on birth control. What sixteen year old girl these days isn't?" His voice had gone up with each word and other kids were staring at them now, other kids who thought they were having a fight, other girls who would be glad they were no longer together, because then Brad might date them.

He tore away from her and began to walk away. She called his name but he didn't look back.

A blond in her lit class brushed by her and murmured, "Breaking up? That's tough."

Word would spread about what had happened. She didn't think anyone had been within earshot to hear about her being pregnant, but she never knew. And even if no one had heard, in a few months, everyone would know. What was she going to do?

The breakfast smells of scrambled eggs and bacon, along with coffee, filled Clare's small house, as she hurried down the hall to rap on Shara's door again Tuesday morning. She'd done that once earlier...before she'd assembled breakfast and called to her daughter. She hadn't heard a reply but that wasn't unusual.

She and Shara had had more than one go-around over the weekend about cutting class. Clare had threatened to pack up the desktop computer sitting in Shara's room and give it to Goodwill. It was a bit of a dinosaur, but it still worked for what Shara needed. Clare had passed it down when she'd gotten her laptop.

Shara had looked wild-eyed and panicked at Clare's threat, mumbling about not being able to do the schoolwork she did have. So Clare had hesitated. Why did she never know exactly what to do?

Breakfast was usually cereal or toast. Had she felt guilty she'd been so angry lately? And cooking put her in a better mommy league?

When Clare opened Shara's door, she didn't see her daughter right away, but that didn't concern her. Maybe Shara was digging in her closet for something to wear today. The covers were thrown back on the bed as if she'd just climbed out.

"Shara?"

No answer. The closet door was open, but Shara was nowhere to be found.

Where was she?

Clare's gaze automatically went to the small step stool shaped like a cat that her mother had given Shara when she was three. That's where her backpack usually landed. There was no backpack there. Had she already left for school without saying anything? She might do that if she was angry and rebelling.

Warning herself to stay calm, Clare wished she let Shara have a phone. But she hadn't wanted the extra expense. Besides, she'd seen a phone as a privilege Shara had to earn and she hadn't yet.

Going to the closet, immediately Clare saw Shara's newest pair of sneakers were missing. She was probably wearing those. But her cowboy boots were gone, too.

A tremble of fear crawling up her spine, Clare went through Shara's clothes. She knew them by heart. She was in this closet more than her daughter was, cleaning it out, hanging up laundry, looking for anything that wasn't appropriate. She'd become the fashion police lately.

Her breath caught when she realized a pair of jeans were missing, the ones with the embroidered pockets. So were the ones Clare knew had holes in them. A pair of khakis she'd bought a few weeks ago along with a red blouse were missing, too. Over-the-top scared now, Clare went to the drawer where Shara kept sports clothes. A pair of sweats and a few T-shirts were gone.

Gone.

Gone...just like Lynnie.

No. This was not happening again. Wherever Shara was, Clare suspected she'd gone of her own free will. There was one place to start, the Hansen household. But after she dialed the number and paced, no one picked up. She didn't have a cell number.

School. If she waited forty-five minutes, she could check and see if Shara was in homeroom. Maybe she just wanted to give her mom a scare. But then why were clothes missing?

Should she wait the forty-five minutes or call someone? But who would she call? She remembered Joe saying she could call him. Call now? Wait?

She couldn't go to work, not like this. She'd phone her supervisor and wait to call the school.

Forty-five minutes later, Clare discovered Shara had been marked absent from her homeroom. She dialed Joe's number. He sounded wide awake when he answered and she suspected he was an early riser. She said, "It's Clare. Shara's missing. I called the school and she's not there. I don't know what to do."

"I'll be right there."

And he was, but she didn't feel any less terrified. She didn't feel any more reassured. He was dressed in a casual shirt and jeans and wore a worried expression. "What's missing from her room?"

Clare told him, again listing each item.

He said, "Let's see what else is gone. We might be able to tell how long she planned to be away."

How long she planned to be away? Clare hadn't even guessed this might be a permanent decision on Shara's part. Oh Lord, what had she done?

"I went too far last night. I told her I'd take her computer if she didn't shape up."

He clasped Clare's elbow. "Slow down. She's a teenager. You have no idea what she was thinking. If she took all the clothes you said, she had to put them in something. Does she have a duffel?"

"No, just her backpack. Unless…" Clare quickly rushed through the kitchen to the laundry room and the storage closet there. She pulled it open. "My travel bag is missing."

"I don't think she took that to school," Joe muttered.

"Should I call the police?" She remembered how soon they'd descended on the household when they'd called about Lynnie.

"She's sixteen. My guess is they'll consider her a runaway. I know you've been through this before," he said with some compassion, "And so have your parents. I really think you should call one of them and get their advice."

She didn't want to, oh, how she didn't want to. But she had to put aside her own sense of independence. She had to put aside the relationship she didn't have with her parents. This was all about Shara and she had to do what was best for her.

Clare called her dad.

When her father walked in, all over again Clare felt as if she was a little girl who had done something wrong. At her age, she knew better. She knew she wasn't responsible for Lynnie's disappearance. But she *was* responsible for being the daughter who was left, the daughter who reminded her mom and dad that they'd lost their youngest, the daughter who could never make up for that.

Trying to keep some semblance of normalcy, she introduced Joe. Her dad had never met him, though her mom had one day when Joe was trimming the bushes in his yard and her mom had stopped over for a picnic supper. But her dad didn't seem to care about social niceties. He nodded to Joe, looked him over with a father's eye and an expression that wondered if the two of them were involved. But he didn't ask. Rather, he shot questions at her...just like a lawyer. "Is there any sign of forced entry? Did she crawl out the window or go out the front door? Are you sure you didn't hear anything? What time frame are we dealing with? What was the time you saw her last night? You didn't check on her before you called for her this morning? Tell me exactly what's missing."

"I don't know how she left. I checked on her last night around ten. This morning I called her for breakfast and when she didn't come—" Clare's voice cracked.

Her father canvassed Shara's room as if he were searching for that one important clue...as if Clare hadn't done that already.

"And you really have no idea where she went?"

"Her friends are in school. I can't talk to them until they're out. I didn't call you over here to give me the third degree. I thought you'd know the next best thing to do. Maybe I should have called Mom."

"I'm just trying to get to the bottom of what happened here," Max snapped, his voice gruff.

"No, what you're doing is remembering, and you're blaming me for Shara running away just like you blamed me for Lynnie running away."

Max looked stunned...as if she'd slapped him. Maybe she'd *intended* her words to be a shock. Maybe she'd finally intended to get it all out in the open. Yet she could see from his closed face that that wasn't going to happen. Although her father was a lawyer, he talked to people rather than listening to them. Maybe that wasn't true with his clients and their parents, but it was true with his family.

Max cut a glance to Joe. "This isn't a conversation for right now."

"It hasn't been a conversation at all for the past twenty-seven years, but we can move on. I know the first few hours are important...so important."

Her father didn't come closer to comfort her. He didn't fling his arm around her neck, something he'd never done again after Lynnie was abducted. But he did gentle his voice. "I'm going to contact a veteran on the police force who was a rookie and there when Lynnie was abducted. We *will* get to the bottom of this, Clare. We'll find Shara. Now why don't you call your mom. She'll be horribly upset if we don't let her know what's happened."

Her mother *was* going to be horribly upset. But Clare went to the phone anyway, knowing she had no choice but to call and give her mother bad news.

As Amanda let herself into Clare's house, she was somewhere between stunned horror and tears. Yet she knew Max hated the tears. Shara was missing. Missing.

Yet this was different from what had happened to Lynnie, she told herself. So different. Shara had probably left of her own accord.

However, when Amanda saw the expression on her daughter's face, she knew Clare was feeling everything she herself had felt so many years ago. Her daughter was stiff, resisting, holding herself tightly together, just like Amanda had done.

Clare motioned to Joe. "I called him because I didn't know what else to do. He suggested I call you and dad...since you'd been through it before."

In spite of the turmoil Amanda felt at the thought of Shara being out in the world alone, she knew it was telling that Clare had called Joe. Did she depend on him? Might they be involved?

Amanda found herself hoping they were, though Clare had never given any indication of that. Her daughter needed something special in her life...*someone* special.

There was another man in the room, too, dressed in a suit. Amanda suspected who *he* was.

Max took over the introductions this time. "This is Detective Sergeant Hobart."

Amanda extended her hand, thinking the detective appeared a bit familiar. She guessed he was in his late forties, with sandy blond hair and a midriff that might be proof he'd eaten too many donuts. He had a round face and blue eyes and tortoise shell glasses. Those glasses rang a bell, too.

"We met a long time ago," he said to Amanda. "I was a rookie working on your daughter's case."

"You worked with Detective Grove?"

"Yes, I did. Not his right-hand man or anything. Mostly ran errands then, took calls on the hotline. That type of thing."

"Have you found out anything about Shara?"

"No ma'am, not yet. I'm doing this as a favor for your husband. At sixteen, well the truth is, we usually give it twenty-four hours because sometimes they do come home. It's not like with—" He stopped abruptly.

"You can say it," Amanda assured him, being strong, showing Max she could be. "Lynnie didn't leave of her own free will. Shara probably did." Her gaze went to Clare but her daughter looked away. She was pale and drawn and Amanda could only imagine the emotions roiling inside of her.

"I was just about to ask your daughter a few more questions," Hobart said.

Amanda knew all about questions, thousands of them, most of them having no answers.

The detective asked Clare, "Did you daughter have access to any money?"

"If she had any, it wasn't much. She'd just had a shopping spree at the mall. I made her take a few things back. It would have been less than a hundred dollars."

He frowned. "That would be her own money. I was thinking more of *your* money. Have you checked your wallet?"

"Shara would never—"

"Ms. Thaddeus, kids who want to run away do lots of things you wouldn't expect. You said she's not on drugs or drinking to your knowledge, but that doesn't mean she's not going to pull from any resources she can. Do you mind checking your wallet, and any place you might keep some funds?"

Amanda wanted to hold Clare and comfort her as she saw understanding sweep through her. But she was Max's daughter clear through, independent and rebellious. That might hold her in good stead right now.

Without another word, Clare went to the freezer.

Max began, "The detective asked you to check your purse."

"I know, Dad, I'm checking something else first. Shara knows I keep extra money in a zip-lock bag wrapped in foil in the freezer. So just back off a bit until—" She reached her hand into side of the freezer and along a pack of frozen bacon. She pulled out a zip-lock bag with a slim foil package inside. She took out the foil package, hoping the bills were still there. They weren't. Her gaze met the detective's. "There was probably about three hundred dollars in here. It's gone."

His voice was soothing. "You have to remember, that for whatever reason, she might have been desperate."

"She didn't have to be desperate. She has *me*." Clare's emotions shook in her voice and now Amanda did go to her and take her hand.

"We'll find out what's going on with Shara. We'll find her. You have to believe that."

"Oh, Mom, how can I?"

"Check your wallet," Max said in a gruff voice.

Amanda could have socked him. For once in his life, couldn't he just show a little compassion? She gave him a glance that said exactly what she was thinking.

His face reddened a little, but he didn't back down. "We have to know how far she can get. We don't even know if she ran off by herself, or if she's with someone else."

Hobart said, "I'll be stopping over at the school when I'm finished here. I'll check if Brad Hansen is there. If he is, I'll question him. If he isn't, I'll let you know."

Clare's movements seemed almost robotic as she went to the counter and unzipped her hobo purse. After she pulled out her wallet, she checked the contents. White-faced, she leaned against the counter. "My ATM card's gone and so is one of my credit cards."

Amanda's heart sank along with her daughter's. With what she'd taken, Shara could go farther than any of them had thought possible.

Chapter Five

After the detective left—Joe had excused himself before the questioning began—Amanda had wandered into Shara's bedroom. He'd reassured them that often teens decided against being on their own and returned that night. Yet from the questions he'd asked and the evidence of the money, the credit card and the bank card that was missing along with Shara, Amanda knew he didn't believe that any more than they did. She couldn't stand any more of the police talk, the questions, the underlying insinuation that as a parent, you'd done something wrong.

Had Clare done something wrong? From the story that had come out about what had happened with this Brad Hansen in the past week, it just sounded as if Shara didn't want to abide by Clare's rules. But who knew what was going on in a young girl's mind?

As Amanda sank down onto Shara's bed, she scanned the room that was so totally her granddaughter's. She didn't have teen idols on her walls. No, she seemed to go for older men. Because she'd never had a father? Because Max hadn't been present in her life any more than he had in Clare's? The poster was Alex O'Loughlin from Hawaii Five-O. Good looking and sexy. Hot.

Since when had Amanda thought in those terms? Not in years. All that had ended with Max leaving. She had no desire to go to the church's social next Thursday, or the community's single parent get-togethers. No, she had her business. At home, she had hobbies. She only wished Clare let her into her life more completely.

And if Lynnie was found? What difference would that make to their family?

Lynnie. Shara. It all swirled in Amanda's head.

Max found her sitting there, thinking about the past as much as the present.

"This isn't going to be the same," he said in a grim voice, as if he could fathom exactly what she was thinking. "Shara's not three. She has a free will and a loud enough mouth when she wants it to be. She took off and somehow we'll find her, but that doesn't mean she's going to want to come back."

Gazing up at Max, Amanda felt her heart fill up with sudden anger. "And why *wouldn't* she want to come back?"

"Clare has the answer to that. I don't."

She was already shaking her head. "That's not true, Max. We *all* have the answer. You and I split and created a separation that hurt everyone. Clare became pregnant because of it. She had Shara to prove a point. Even when Shara's dad skipped town and was never heard from again, Clare took very little assistance from us because she wants distance between us. Distance is what caused this problem. If we'd been here, *really* been here, to support her in raising Shara, maybe this never would have happened." She knew there was accusation in her tone and recrimination in her eyes, but she couldn't help it.

"Don't get side-tracked into the past again, Amanda. You live in that shop and you spend too much time there. Moving forward is the only way to go, and we will move forward with this. The detective's doing his part unofficially and we're going to do ours. When more time goes by, he'll make this an official investigation."

Max went over to Shara's computer and booted it up. "He's not going to be interested in this until he gets his preliminary questions asked and interviews kids at the school. In the meantime, I'm going to see what I can find out."

"On her computer?"

"Kids live on these things now, along with their phones. I wish Clare would have let Shara have one because maybe then we could trace her. Since she doesn't have one, I'll see what her computer files can tell us."

If Max didn't have something to do, he was lost. He couldn't sit still. He couldn't just be. That had been a big problem between them—not insurmountable until Lynnie had been taken. Then Max was out in his car, driving road after road, or at the police station, or talking to search parties, or having flyers printed, or finding money for a reward.

"Clare," he called in that determined, authoritarian voice that Amanda knew turned Clare off.

But their daughter came running in. "Did you find something?"

"Not yet, but I will. I need your help getting into the computer. What's Shara's password?"

"I don't know."

"What do you mean you don't know?"

"When I handed down the desktop to Shara, I let her choose her password."

"Don't you check what she's doing on here?"

"Once in a while. I ask her to log in and then I fish around. But I didn't want to invade her privacy."

"Because of that, she could easily have five thousand dollars at her disposal and flee anywhere. You should have been monitoring her closely."

"She's sixteen, Dad. If I did that, she wouldn't even go on this computer. She has to know I have some degree of trust in her."

"And where did that get you?"

Amanda raised her hand and waved it between the two of them. "Stop! Please. The idea is to work on this together." She looked at Max. "Don't make things worse."

"How can it be any worse?" he asked her.

"We can lose Clare, too," she said clearly and succinctly, reminding him he still had a daughter who mattered. Neither of them had remembered that soon enough after Lynnie had been taken.

Clare looked near tears. Amanda stood, put her own feelings aside, put the tension with Max aside and hung her arm around Clare's shoulders. She gave her a squeeze. "We'll figure this out. Can you make a list of Shara's favorite things, favorite words she uses, anything like that that she might use as a password."

"Even if we figure out this password," Clare said, "she has different ones for different sites. She used to have a small Rolodex so she wouldn't forget them. If we could find that—" She glanced at her father. "She doesn't leave it out on her desk when she's not here because she doesn't want me snooping, so obviously there's a hiding place."

Decidedly frustrated, Max ran his hand through his hair. "All right, then we tear up the room. We find that Rolodex."

They went through the room, inch by inch. At least they thought they did. Clare took the dresser drawers. Amanda searched through the chest. Max looked everywhere else.

"This room isn't that big," he muttered. "It has to be somewhere."

"It wouldn't make sense that she took it with her," Clare said. "She left in a hurry and she might not have even remembered it."

After forty-five minutes of looking in every nook and cranny, they glanced at each other in frustration.

"Would she have hidden it somewhere else?" Amanda asked.

"I doubt it. Shara's room is her island, the place she goes to get away from me and everyone else."

"I should have kept in touch with her more," Amanda murmured. "If she wouldn't talk to you, maybe she would have talked with me."

"Mom, don't pull the guilt trip again. Please."

Amanda was startled by her daughter's words.

"Clare," Max warned.

But apparently Clare was tired of keeping her thoughts and feelings bottled up. "I mean it. After Lynnie was gone, you two were so filled with guilt, I couldn't stand to be in the room with you. Don't do that now. If anyone should feel guilty, it's me. But I don't have time for self-pity. We have to find her."

Self-pity. Is that what she and Max had indulged in? Was that the biggest obstacle that had shut Clare out? Maybe it wasn't the search, the phone calls, the police intervention. Maybe it had been their own attitudes toward their daughter. Why couldn't parents and kids figure this out? Why was communication so tough when they had so many words at their disposal? Communication with her husband hadn't been any easier than communication with her daughter. She just couldn't let the same barriers they had erected before become barriers again.

Amanda sat on the bed and patted the place next to her. "Come here a minute, Clare."

Clare eyed her warily. "Why?"

"Let's just breathe for a couple of minutes and talk."

Max made a move to leave the room.

"You, too," she suggested. "We all need to think about our teen-age years, what was important to us, who we told things to and where we hid things."

Although she seemed unsure, Clare crossed the room and sat beside her mother. The mere six inches between them seemed like the world, but Amanda forged ahead anyway. Her focus switched to her husband. "When you were a teen-ager, where did you put anything you didn't want your dad to find?"

"He never looked in my room. He didn't care what I had hidden unless it was a bottle of whiskey."

Clare's head snapped up. "Whiskey?"

At first Max looked as if he wanted to close down. Amanda knew that was her husband's way of dealing with his emotions. But as he studied his daughter, the curiosity and sadness in her eyes, he pulled out Shara's desk chair and lowered himself into it.

"You were too young to remember," Max said, as if that were explanation enough.

"Remember what? That Grandpa drank?"

"We didn't visit him when you were a baby because he was rarely sober. I spent my life trying to escape everything he represented."

The problem was, after hope for finding Lynnie had died, Max had fallen on his father's habits.

His gaze met Amanda's, held for a few moments, then glanced away. "Your mom and I divorced in part because I started drinking."

"Dad!" Clare's voice was a breathy wisp.

"I hid it well, most of the time, especially when you were around. But your mom, she knew what my dad had been and she didn't want me turning into him."

"You could never…" Amanda began.

He put up a hand to stop her. "You don't know that." He explained to Clare. "My dad was a mean drunk."

"He abused you?" Clare asked, horrified.

"Not after I got big enough to defend myself. I got very good at defending myself. When he learned I wouldn't back down, *he* did. He was essentially a bully and bullies really don't like facing strength."

"Grandpa died suddenly," Clare remembered.

"It might have seemed sudden to you, but it wasn't. He died of cirrhosis, mainly because he wouldn't let anybody help him."

"Did you let someone help *you*? You're not drinking now, are you?" She sounded horrified that he might be.

"No, I'm not drinking now. A friend helped me. When I was at my lowest, about a year after your mom and I divorced, he dragged me to an AA meeting."

"You go to AA?"

"I do. I've been sober for twenty-four years, but I still need meetings now and then."

What hurt Amanda most was that Max hadn't let *her* help him. He hadn't let her intervene. But then maybe he just hadn't been ready...or maybe it had just hurt too much to look her in the eyes and remember what had happened to Lynnie.

"Why didn't you tell me any of this before?" Clare asked, looking hurt.

Max shrugged. "What would that have helped?"

"I would have understood you better. I might have understood the divorce better."

"The divorce had nothing to do with you," he maintained.

"No child believes that," Clare said. "I blamed myself for Lynnie's abduction and I blamed myself for your divorce."

"Oh, Clare." Amanda hung her arm around Clare's shoulders, but Clare shrugged it off.

"I don't know why you're so surprised, Mom. You hardly paid any attention to me. You were so sad all the time."

Yes, she had been, and some of that sadness still remained. She doubted if it would ever go away. She wanted to say, *Think about Shara. What if you never saw her again? What kind of black hole would that create in your heart?* But she couldn't do that to Clare. She and Max had done enough.

Yet Clare must have realized what she'd been thinking because a terrified look came into her eyes. "What if I never see her again?"

"That's not going to happen," Max maintained again. "We're going to figure this out." He stared at Amanda. "Where did you keep anything you didn't want your parents to find?"

Amanda thought about it. "Our farmhouse had a huge attic. We stored everything up there—some furniture, old clothes, the Christmas decorations. There was this old trunk there that belonged to my grandmother. Basically it was filled with blankets and scarves, crocheted doilies. That type of thing. I buried my diary in one of the corners under all of it. That felt safe."

Clare was looking at her mom as if she'd never seen her before. "You kept a diary?"

"Doesn't every young girl? Maybe now you call them journals and you do them on-line, but it's pretty much the same thing. So now, tell me, where did you hide things from me and your dad?"

"Under a loose floorboard in my closet."

"You had loose floorboards?" Max asked.

"With a little prying. You know, they didn't quite meet the wall. It wasn't hard."

Max glanced at the floor and the carpeting there, then he looked toward the closet. " Let's give her closet another go. I'll check the corners to see if the carpet comes up."

The three of them emptied Shara's closet. Clare hoisted the hangers with clothes over her shoulder and carried them to the bed. Max piled shoe boxes on top of each other and pushed them outside the closet while Amanda reached to clear the top shelf that ran along the length of the closet above the clothes bar. But after Clare sneezed from the dust they'd raised, after Max had studied each corner and found the carpet still attached to the stripping around the edges while Amanda held her breath and hoped, they found nothing.

"This could be useless," Max said. "She could have buried it outside for all we know."

"No," Clare mused. "That's too noticeable if she wanted to fetch it. It has to be in this room. She wouldn't want it very far from her computer."

Amanda gazed upward and suddenly realized the ceiling in the closet, unlike the ceiling in the bedroom, which was drywall or something like it, was composed of ceiling tiles. She gestured to it. "Those push up, don't they?"

Max looked up and then down at the floor. "They certainly do. That's so the electricians can get to the electrical work." He clasped Amanda's shoulder. "You're a genius."

The touch of Max's hand through her sweater sent warmth through her, warmth she hadn't felt in a very long time. His praise shouldn't mean so much, but she found it still did. That feeling unsettled her. She'd moved well on from their marriage. She'd become a different person and she suspected he had, too. So there was no place for that tightness in the middle of her chest, that little giddy tummy-twirl, that chemistry they'd both felt when they were teenagers.

Already he was moving into the bedroom, heading for the desk chair.

Amanda's shoulder brushed Clare's as they moved to the side for Max to push the chair in and then climb up on it. It was unusual to be this close to Clare. Usually her daughter shrugged away. She just hated that the price of the closeness was these circumstances.

Max was an organized man, a lawyer, and he knew how to do a search. He started in the right corner, lifting one tile at a time, carefully feeling around the raised tile, and along the metal strips.

"Damn," he muttered at one point and Amanda suspected what had happened. She rushed from the closet, went to the bathroom, and grabbed a box of bandages. She knew Clare always kept a filled box out of habit because Shara had been a rough and tumble kid, always scraping something. Little Shara had been a joy—open, friendly, loving. But as she'd become a preteen and then a teenager, she'd become more sullen, more alienated, more stand-offish. Amanda had always felt that her granddaughter loved her, but as a developing young woman, just didn't know how to show it. At that age, hormones could take the place of good sense. At any age, really. Sometimes she wondered if the lack of them now in her own body caused overreactions as much as the over-abundance of them when she was a teenager.

When she tapped Max's arm, he looked down. Seeing the bandage in her hand, he shook his head. "I'm fine."

"You don't want to bleed all over Clare's ceiling tiles. Take thirty seconds and put it on."

She could see he was about to refuse, about to lift the next ceiling tile, when his gaze settled on hers and they both went perfectly still. He reached down and took the bandage from her fingers. She took the wrapper from him as he applied it.

"Thanks," he said, looking as if he meant it.

She didn't say anything as he went back to his search. But when she glanced at Clare, she saw her daughter looking at her with curiosity, as if maybe she sensed that something unusual had happened.

After readjusting the chair three times, Max felt in the farthest left corner up above the shelf. "I've got something," he said, and Amanda's heart thumped wildly. First, he pulled down a pale pink diary that had one of those clasps with a small lock. He handed it down to Clare.

"I gave her this when she was ten," Clare said. "I doubt if she writes in it now. It's not locked." Without hesitating, she opened the clasp and shuffled to the last page. "The last entry's three years ago."

She closed it again as Max felt along the wider side

strip at the edge of the closet ceiling. Triumphantly he pulled out a small Rolodex and held it up for them to see.

"Now, we're making progress."

Amanda hoped that Rolodex held the answer to their prayers.

Chapter Six

Once at Shara's desk, Clare stepped aside and let her dad sit at the computer. After all, she should have been doing this before now. She should have monitored Shara better. She should have known what was in her daughter's head.

He flipped through the Rolodex quickly, getting an overview of the type of passwords Shara used and the sites she visited.

"Do you know anything about *Branches*?" Max asked, looking up at Clare.

"No, I've never heard of it."

"She doesn't have an icon for it on the desktop which makes me think she didn't want you to see it. But there's a password. Let's see what we can find."

"Do you know anything about this site?" she asked.

"It's come up."

With her dad's association with family law, she imagined it might be relevant in lots of ways. "Is it something bad?"

"It's what the kids make it. It's a social media site that's grown in popularity."

From the search engine, he accessed the site. From the information on the card in the Rolodex, he signed in with Shara's user name and password. Her page came up.

Max whistled through his teeth. "Our granddaughter thinks she's twenty-five instead of sixteen. Unfortunately she doesn't have the good sense to know the difference. My God, what was she thinking?"

Clare was almost afraid to look, but she did.

There was a photo of Shara in a bathing suit Clare had never seen. Actually it couldn't even be called a bathing suit. It was definitely a skimpy bikini. The poses weren't sweet, but rather suggestive. Whatever she was trying to do, she was absolutely giving off the wrong message. That was obvious by the comments on her page, most of them from guys. Clare wasn't naïve, and she suspected many of the males behind the messages were a lot older than they pretended to be.

She was still looking over her father's shoulder, becoming more and more appalled, listening to her mom's equally upset comments, when her father said, "One guy here is commenting more than the others. He doesn't seem to be as sleazy, but my guess is that's just a pretense. I don't trust male motives on a site like this. Who knows? His name's Justin. Ever heard Shara mention him?"

"No, she's never mentioned anyone but Brad."

"This back and forth has been going on for a while. From what I can tell from her timeline, maybe about ten months. It's sporadic at first, but they're definitely flirting, bantering back and forth, like high schoolers do. Yet he sounds more mature than a high schooler. He mentions here that he would e-mail her. Let's check her e-mails."

"Dad."

Max's reaction was quick and repudiating. "You want to find out where your daughter is, don't you?"

Her mother laid a quieting hand on her father's shoulder, and Clare just stared at them in a flash of insight struck by the history they shared. What was it like for her mom to touch her dad when they'd been divorced for so long? What was it like for them to be here in the same room, worrying again, when they weren't even together for holidays any more?

"Of course, I want to find her," she murmured. Then she added, "But I keep hoping she'll call or something. Why would she let me worry like this?"

"She's rebelling and she's angry," Amanda responded. "She's probably angry at the world as much as at you. There had to be some kind of incident that made her run. We have to find out what it was."

Clare hadn't realized how wise her mother had become over the years. Maybe it was all the counseling she'd had. Maybe it was the sheer experience of losing a daughter. Whatever it was, Clare was grateful for her insight now.

She added some of her own.

"It must have been something to do with Brad."

Max exited *Branches*, clicked on the icon for Shara's e-mail program and found her user name and password in the Rolodex.

Her father seemed to know exactly what he was doing, so Clare asked, "Have you done this before?"

"Try to find someone's daughter or son, husband or
wife? Usually I have a private investigator to do this kind
of thing, but I've learned a trick or two myself. Everyone
sloughs off e-mails as if they're disposable, and they are if
you do it right. But most people don't. They just delete
them from their in-box and think they're gone, or delete
them from their trash and don't clean out their recycle
bins. Real criminals, frauds or perverts are more careful
about it. But Shara doesn't fall into any of those catego-
ries, so my guess is she wasn't careful. She thinks she hid
her passwords, but the truth is, even those can be broken
with the right programs. Let's see what we've got."

As they all peered at the monitor, Max dismissed
the e-mails from classmates. After he went through the
In-box list, he switched to the Trash. "Here we are. Justin. His handle is 1234. But I don't recognize the server.
One of my paralegals at the office is good at this kind
of thing. I'll put her on it."

Taking out his phone, he sent a text message, got a
quick response, and went back to what he was doing.
Clare had already been looking over the last e-mail.

"Oh my gosh, Dad, he sounds so sympathetic. He's
telling her everything she wants to hear."

"Yeah, that's what predators do."

Clare felt her heart practically stop. A predator lur-
ing her daughter. That just couldn't be.

They swiftly went through more e-mails and then
Max spotted the one that gave them the information
they needed.

"Sandia Peak. That's Albuquerque. He's telling her she should come to Albuquerque for a break." Pushing himself away from the desk, Max announced, "I'm going to Albuquerque."

Although Clare was glad they'd found a lead and her dad was doing something, she exchanged a look with her mom. "But you don't know where to go. You don't even know his last name."

"Hopefully I'll get his last name when we trace his IP address."

Amanda said quietly, "But what if he's using a fake name? It's like all the leads with Lynnie—"

"Don't even say it," Max snapped. "Do *not* say it."

After a strained moment of silence, Amanda said off-handedly, "If you're going to Albuquerque, I'm going with you."

"Amanda—"

"Don't use that authoritarian voice with me, Max. Don't argue with me. I won't change my mind."

"I should go, too," Clare stated.

But her father disagreed. "No, you shouldn't. You need to stay here in case we're all wrong about this. You need to be here if Shara comes back home. You need to be in touch with the police department here."

She wanted to fight what her dad was saying. She wanted to go searching for her daughter. Was it a wiser strategy to stay here and wait?

The doorbell rang. Amanda suggested, "Maybe that's the detective."

Clare rushed to the front door. Amanda was on her way there, too, when she recognized the sound of the visitor. It was Joe. Maybe he could be some kind of consolation to Clare. She doubted if she and Max could be.

Max must have recognized his voice, too, because he turned back to the desktop, studied the e-mails once more and took out his cell phone. "I'm going to get us seats on the next flight out."

"We don't know what we're doing," Amanda said calmly, having her own ideas about what they should do. She had to make Max listen.

"We know this Justin is in Albuquerque and he invited Shara to visit him. By the time we get there, maybe we'll have more information about him."

"And maybe we won't."

"What are you suggesting? I'm not staying here when I have a lead."

"I'm suggesting we call Gillian Bradley."

Max went perfectly still. "You're not going to pull me into that woo-hoo universe again. She couldn't help the last time we called her."

After Lynnie had been taken, and no leads panned out, Amanda had consulted a couple of psychics. None of them had provided useful information though they were willing to take money for trying. Then year before last, still desperately needing to know what had happened to her daughter no matter what that was, Amanda had found a blog online. Gillian Bradley had found a child who had been lost while the family had been camping near Big Sur. Full of hope, Amanda had told Max about her. Still leery about treading in those murky waters, he'd agreed to consult with her and they'd flown to California. In spite of Gillian's impressive success rate, she'd come up blank. She'd gotten nowhere.

"This situation with Shara is different," Amanda insisted. "Even if Shara ran to Albuquerque to be with this Justin, hopefully nothing has happened yet. She's just running. Now's the time to find out if Gillian can get a bead on her."

"Oh, Amanda."

"You know a foundation funds Gillian and her partner. She still helps even if someone can't pay daily expenses."

"Rich people donate and pay her salary." He checked his watch. "I just want to make those airline reservations."

"Don't close down on me, Max. Haven't you done that enough over the years?"

"So now it's another guilt trip?"

Amanda sighed. "No, but I'll use whatever I can to get you to try every avenue. We're not going to let what happened to Lynnie happen to Shara."

At that moment, Max looked weary, as if all these past years of searching drew lines in his face at the same time. He closed his eyes, opened them again and then maybe really saw her for the first time in years.

"All right, call Gillian Bradley. But don't expect too much out of it, Amanda. She might be too busy to even consider helping us. She might not even be searching for missing persons any more."

That was possibly true, but Amanda didn't think so. Gillian had a gift and if Amanda had read her right, she wouldn't put it aside if she could help others.

Joe had brought take-out from Happy Family, the Chinese restaurant downtown. He said seriously, "I know no one's thinking about food, or thinking they want any food, but believe me, you've all got to keep your strength up." He carried the bags to the kitchen table and Clare followed him.

"You didn't have to do this."

"I know. I wanted to."

He looked at her as if he wanted to bring her more than lunch, and Clare couldn't deal with that right now, so she looked away.

But he wasn't the type of man to allow that. After setting the bags on the table, he came close and lifted her chin, forcing their gazes to meet. "Don't shut me out. You need a friend right now."

"A friend?"

"We'll discuss what we're going to be after this is all over," he decided.

"Will it be all over? It never has been with my sister."

"Ah, Clare, you have to think positive."

"I'm trying. And we did find something." She told him about their search, *Branches*, and the e-mails her father had unearthed. "Mom and Dad are flying to Albuquerque. I don't know what to do. They say I should stay here. And I wonder what they're going to be able to do *there*?"

"I think since your sister was taken, all three of you have tried to stand on your own, haven't you?"

"I *had* to stand on my own. My parents weren't

there for me while I was growing up. They weren't there for me when I got pregnant."

"Did they want to be?"

Joe asked the difficult questions. Maybe her parents had wanted to be her support, and she'd been too defiant and resentful to let them.

"Even if I accept their help, I don't know if they're going to accept each other's. Sure, they have a common goal, but that old tension is still there between them. It started the night Lynnie disappeared and it's always been there. It contributed to their divorce. And now—"

"Now, they have a common goal again," he said.

"But that won't change who they are. That won't change how they feel about what happened in the past. I learned today that Dad started drinking after Lynnie disappeared, and that's one of the reasons he and Mom divorced."

"Is he drinking now?"

"No. Maybe that's why Mom has insisted she's going with him, so he doesn't. I don't know."

Stepping closer, keeping his eyes on hers, he took her by the shoulders. "You can't solve your parents' problems, but you can let them help you. You can be here for Shara. You've got to keep the best possible outlook on this, not the worst, and you'll be able to keep in touch with your parents to know what's happening every step of the way. That's what cell phones and texting are for, right?"

Thinking about it, Clare found herself biting her lower lip, feeling younger than she was, feeling uncertain about everything.

"Your parents probably don't know how much they hurt you. Have you ever told them?"

She'd let a little of that come out today. Still … "How could I tell them when they were hurting so badly because Lynnie was gone. I let some of my feelings slip today. They seemed shocked, actually shocked. Are they really so clueless?"

"They're human, Clare. They've tried to do their best, but that just wasn't enough with you. You have to decide if you're going to forgive them and move out of this, or if you're always going to hold bitterness toward them."

She saw the look in his eyes and the road she should take. "You're going to tell me bitterness is only going to hurt *me*, not them."

"No, I'm not. It will hurt all of you."

His eyes were so kind and compassionate that she found tears coming to hers. Blinking hard, she tried to turn away. But instead of letting her, he pulled her into a hug and he held her tight.

"Mrs. Bradley, I don't know if you remember me. I'm Amanda Thaddeus. My husband and I met with you about trying to find our daughter Lynnie." In spite of her efforts to stay calm, Amanda's voice shook.

"Of course, I remember you. I wasn't able to help you. Please, call me Gillian."

"I hope it's okay that I called your home number rather than the foundation's number. You had given it to me and—"

Home for Gillian Bradley was near L.A. Amanda remembered the Spanish house in the hills, the welcoming feel of it when she and Max had traveled there.

"This number's fine. Has something happened? Have you gotten a lead?"

"Actually we have. We don't know if anything will come of it, but that's not why I'm calling. My granddaughter has run away. We don't know why, but she made a friend on-line through *Branches*, and we think she's gone to visit him in Albuquerque. We don't know anything else. We're trying to trace his IP because they e-mailed back and forth, but we want to find her before something happens to her. Can you help?"

When there wasn't an immediate response, Amanda said, "We're flying to Albuquerque as soon as we can get a flight. The police are on this, but, well, you know how I feel about that."

"What's your granddaughter's name?"

"It's Shara—Shara Thaddeus. Clare was never married."

"If I remember correctly, your husband wasn't too keen on enlisting my help the first time."

"He's my ex-husband," Amanda reminded her, "And he really has no choice this time. I'm not going to sit by without doing everything I can."

"Shara," Gillian said thoughtfully.

Amanda had no idea whether Gillian was considering helping them or not. Did she get a feeling just from a name? "Can we send you something? Do I need to come see you?" That's what they'd done before. She'd taken along clothes of Lynnie's that she'd packed away.

"Albuquerque's on my side of the country. Can you give me a few minutes to call my husband? I'll check out his schedule. I also want to talk to my partner, Jake Donovan."

Amanda remembered Jake. He was a private investigator who did background and research work for Gillian. "Do you want me to hold on?" Amanda asked, hopefully. She couldn't take the chance that Gillian wouldn't call her back.

"No, I have your number from Caller ID. I'll give you a call back in about fifteen minutes. I promise, Amanda, no longer."

There was something in Gillian Bradley's voice that made Amanda believe her.

Fifteen minutes later, Amanda knew what flight they were taking to Albuquerque and the hotel where they'd be staying.

Max asked her, "So you really expect her to call back in fifteen minutes?"

Those fifteen minutes were almost up, but then—

Her cell phone beeped. She saw Gillian's number and gave Max a satisfied nod. "Hello," she said, hoping for the best but expecting the worst. What if Gillian Bradley wouldn't help?

"There are many ways to handle this," Gillian said, "But I think the best is for me to meet you in Albuquerque. When will you be arriving?"

Amanda told her. They were scheduled to arrive there that evening.

"Have you found a hotel?" Gillian asked.

Amanda gave her that information.

"I have a friend, a TV producer, who has access to a charter service and a private jet. I'll make reservations at the hotel."

"You don't know how much I appreciate this!"

"It's what I do, Amanda. I want you to bring some things of Shara's—clothes, jewelry, maybe a pair of shoes, and a picture, perhaps one of when she was small and one of her now. Can you do that?"

"Of course, I can."

"Let me give you my cell number. Is the phone you've been calling me on your cell?"

Gillian covered all the bases and Amanda was glad for that because she was feeling scattered. "Yes."

"Good. Give me a call after you arrive so we can meet up. Does that work for you?"

"That works perfectly. Thank you."

"No thanks necessary. Your daughter's case and my inability to help you has been a regret I haven't been able to forget. I'll see you soon."

As she ended the call, Amanda said a fervent prayer that Gillian would be able to help them this time.

Chapter Seven

For some reason as Amanda walked through Albuquerque International Sunport with Max, she began to feel less depressed. The airport was one of the most artistic and pleasant airports she'd ever been in. Southwest colors, the tile, sculpture hanging from the ceiling and the artwork all around lifted her spirits. She and Max hadn't talked much at all on the drive to BWI airport, on the first flight to Dallas, on the second flight to Albuquerque. Max always withdrew when he was thinking or upset or nervous. *She* liked to talk everything to death. At first that had worked well for them. She drew him out, encouraged him to listen. She'd learned to read body language rather than words, to look into his eyes and learn his truth. They'd even enjoyed silent communication because they'd known each other's hearts and souls.

But now they avoided each other's gazes as they took the shuttle to the rental car facility, as she insisted on taking care of her own bag. They rented a mid-sized

SUV with a GPS and Amanda figured out how to enter the hotel's address into it as Max headed in the right direction. He'd always been good at the logistics of traveling.

At the hotel, they didn't need a bellboy to handle their luggage with only two roll-ons. Amanda knew how to pack light for her antique buying trips. So Max opened the door with his keycard and they entered a small suite.

"You can have the bedroom." Motioning to the sitting area with its sofa, chair and TV, he said, "I'll sleep on the pull out."

She wasn't going to argue with him. He was in that kind of mood.

There was a balcony off the living room area with sliding glass doors that led outside. After she rolled her suitcase into her bedroom and lifted it onto the bed, she took out her cell phone and seemed to gravitate toward that outside terrace. Opening the door, she stepped outside and was greeted by the most beautiful sight in the distance, the Sandia Mountains. They looked pink in the end-of-the-day sunlight as dusk was closing in. Already she liked this city, without knowing exactly why. If she told Max how she felt, he'd scoff. So as she had over the past years, she kept her thoughts to herself as she called Gillian's number. Five minutes later she reluctantly walked back inside. Max was already putting on a pot of coffee to brew.

"Are you hungry?" he asked.

"Gillian will be here in five minutes. We don't have time to eat."

He motioned to the complimentary snacks on the counter. "There are some power bars there. That might hold you over until we can call room service, or grab something in a restaurant."

"I'm not—"

"Don't say it, Amanda. I know you don't want to eat when you're upset. But you have to. You have to keep up your strength for whatever happens next."

Always the pragmatist.

As if he could read her thoughts, he said, "What else can I do but be practical? We're about to meet with a psychic. I need something to balance that."

She almost smiled a little...almost.

Max hefted his suitcase onto the luggage holder near the closet. He'd brought a larger one to fit in everything they'd thrown in of Shara's. Amanda had insisted on bringing more rather than less, intending to help Gillian in whatever way she could.

When there was a rap at the door, she went to answer it. After she looked through the peephole, she recognized the woman she'd met with so hopefully before.

Gillian was in her thirties, with light brown hair. She was slim, wearing jeans, a T-shirt and sandals. Amanda opened the door wide to let her come in.

After she did, Gillian shook both their hands and said, "I'm sorry we have to meet again under these circumstances." Max remained silent as Amanda gestured to the sitting area.

Once Gillian was seated, Max asked gruffly, "What do we have to do this time?"

Gillian looked at him kindly and motioned to the sofa cushions beside her. "Why don't you sit and we'll talk about Shara."

"I don't know what good talking is going to do," he muttered.

Amanda knew what he was thinking. The last time they'd met with Gillian, they'd talked about Lynnie and that hadn't helped. But Gillian insisted, "Talking will give me a sense of her, of your feelings towards her, hers towards you. You said her mother's waiting for word from her at home?"

"I called her as soon as we landed," Amanda said. "No word there. The detective talked to Shara's boyfriend, but he claimed he didn't know anything."

Amanda and Max sat on the long sofa with Gillian beside Amanda. Amanda was so aware of her exhusband beside her, the brush of his jeans against hers, the scent of his after-shave, his broad shoulder almost lodged against hers. Some men as they aged became less of themselves, but Max had become more—more fit, more healthy, more stoic. There was nothing she could do about that last one.

Amanda reached to the coffee table for her purse and pulled a few 4x6 photos from it. She handed them to Gillian. "I thought these would be better than some school photo."

One by one, Gillian studied them. In one photo, Shara stood beside an old-fashioned wooden coat rack with a fedora on her head. "That's in my shop," Amanda explained. "We found the hat in a box with some vintage clothes. She liked it and I told her she could have it."

"Maybe she doesn't need to know all that," Max muttered.

"The more information I have, the better."

Max went silent.

Gillian looked at the next photograph. Amanda had caught this shot of Clare and Shara in Clare's car. That day she was going for her driver's test. Shara had been so excited and trying not to show it.

"Did you go with them that day?" Max asked.

"I did because I insisted they'd both need moral support."

"I didn't even know she'd taken her test."

Amanda wanted to ask—*Whose fault is that?*—but she didn't. She didn't want to start an argument, especially not in front of Gillian. In the last photo, Shara was sitting in an Adirondack chair in her backyard wearing a bathing suit, not the same bathing suit that she'd worn in those pictures on *Branches*.

"She's a beautiful young woman," Gillian said. She ran her fingers over Shara's face in each of the photos, and Amanda felt as if she were holding her breath.

"She's not as free-spirited as she wants everyone to think she is," Gillian mused, "Though she's definitely impulsive."

"Yes, she is," Amanda agreed. "She says it's because she knows what she wants and knows what she thinks. But I believe she just hasn't learned to weigh decisions before she acts."

"Let me see what you brought of hers," Gillian suggested.

Max handed over the grocery bag he'd removed

from his suitcase, and one by one Amanda pulled out the items—a pair of old sneakers, a Ravens' sweatshirt, a pair of denim shorts, a taupe camisole, a school notebook. From a side pocket in her purse, Amanda withdrew a beaded bracelet and a pair of swingy turquoise earrings. She laid them on the coffee table, not knowing what Gillian would want to do with any of it.

Gillian's cell phone rang. It was easy to see Max was annoyed as she pulled it out of her pocket. Checking Caller ID, she took the call with a brief "excuse me" to Amanda and Max.

"Hi, Jake," Amanda heard and realized Gillian was talking to her partner.

"Yes, I understand. That's what we expected. Okay, I know you will. In the meantime, I'll see what I can do. Give my love to Sara and the kids." Turning back to Amanda and Max, she said, "Sorry for the interruption."

"Doesn't taking calls interfere with what you do?" Max asked.

"Max," Amanda chided.

"Its okay, Amanda. Normally I would have put my phone on vibrate, but I was waiting for that call. It was my partner, Jake Donovan. The e-mail address for this Justin is untraceable, at least for now. Apparently the service he uses reroutes it through foreign countries."

"That's what my paralegal said, too," Max said under his breath.

"So let's concentrate on what we can do next."

Gillian took each item they'd brought, held it for a while and considered it. With the earrings, she closed her eyes. Amanda wondered if that's because jewelry was more personal and maybe had a better connection. She wanted to ask because what Gillian did fascinated her, but she didn't want to break any kind of tenuous thread. She didn't want to annoy Max more. She didn't want to postpone whatever Gillian might have to tell them.

When Gillian picked up the bracelet, her expression changed. It was only slight, but Amanda could read something there that hadn't been there before. Gillian closed her eyes again for a few seconds and, beside her, Amanda felt Max get restless. She could feel the tensing in his body. He was about to say something and she didn't want him to, so she pressed her hand to his knee. The jolt of awareness that ran through her arm must have shown in her eyes because his widened in response, too. Couldn't be chemistry, could it? Not after all these years. But there was no doubt she was still attracted to Max. No doubt you couldn't snuff out that kind of attraction easily.

Her touch must have surprised him enough to keep him quiet because his mouth stayed in that very straight line.

Gillian said, "Shara likes jewelry."

"All girls her age like jewelry," Max scoffed, as if he believed this were a cold reading at a Las Vegas show.

His outburst didn't perturb Gillian, though. "Something about Sleeping Beauty turquoise." It was easy to see that the earrings Amanda had brought along were turquoise, and she saw the doubtful clouds grow stormier in Max's eyes.

"Did she ever make jewelry?" Gillian asked.

"No," Amanda said, "Not as far as I know. But I could call Clare and ask."

Gillian shook her head and said, "Let me see where this leads."

Amanda could tell from Max's expression he thought it would lead to the road to nowhere.

Taking the earrings into her hand once more, she ran her thumbs over the wires. Was the DNA on those wires telling her something? Was that what this was all about? Through Shara's DNA, Gillian could sense her?

When Max shifted on the sofa, Amanda gave him another look that told him she expected him to go along with this. She expected him to go along with whatever clues Gillian came up with.

Gillian opened her eyes and shifted her attention to the two of them. "I believe I told you when you met with me before that what I do isn't instantaneous. It's not like I'm a GPS that guides you to where Shara is. But I can tell you what I'm sensing."

"If you can sense anything, that means she's okay, right?" Amanda so wanted to believe that.

"I can't tell you for sure. What I can tell you is that I'm not getting any indication that Shara is bound or tied up or anything violent has happened to her."

"I hear a *but* in there," Max said perceptively.

"But … she *is* scared."

"Scared to come home again?" Amanda asked.

"Scared on many levels. I don't think she's sure she did the right thing, and I also feel—" Gillian stopped. "Never mind about that. We'll pursue that later. But crafting jewelry is foremost in her mind, maybe because she's trying to push some of the other things away."

"She came to Albuquerque to make jewelry?"

"No, she came to be with Justin," Gillian responded. "I'm also sensing one word very strongly—*Zuni*."

"That could mean anything out here," Max said.

"Let's figure out what it could mean," Gillian answered back. "List the possibilities and we'll take them one by one."

He looked at her strangely, but then he complied. "Zuni is a tribe. Even I know that. Do they possibly have land around here?" he asked.

"There's a pueblo about a hundred and fifty miles west of Albuquerque, but I'm not sensing that Shara's in that kind of isolation."

"So you're going to dismiss that?"

"For now, let's explore other possibilities."

"Zuni is a style of jewelry," Amanda said.

"Yes, it is," Gillian agreed. "There *is* another possibility. Zuni could be the name of a street or an apartment complex. Let me explain. I found someone not so long ago because of a pair of twin pines. They stood near arch that led to Twin Pines Ranch. Do you understand the association?"

"So we need a map of Albuquerque to see if there's a Zuni street or something like that." Amanda pulled out her phone. So did Max.

"This is like looking for a needle in a haystack," Max exclaimed.

"And Albuquerque's one big haystack," Amanda agreed.

Gillian's phone rang again. This time Max didn't look annoyed, but expectant.

"What do you have Jake?" she asked her partner.

"His name is Justin Davis," she said in order for them to hear, too. "I'm going to put you on speaker phone."

"Can you hear me?" Jake asked.

"Yes, loud and clear."

"I'm Max, the grandfather. How did you get his name?"

"I have a friend of a friend in *Branches*. Networking is everything in this business."

"What's next?" Max shot back.

"I'm going to search public records to see if he's bought property in Albuquerque, but my guess is, a joker like this rents."

"Rents what?"

"A house, an apartment, a condo. You can bet Shara's probably not the first young woman he's invited to join him, so he's going to careful. He might not want any public records showing his name on them."

"Then how are we going to find him?" Max asked, exasperated.

"With a combination of Gillian's gift and some good old-fashioned detective work. This could take a little time."

"I don't know if we have time," Max warned him.

"Gillian, what's your sense of this?" Jake asked his partner.

"You know I can't be sure, but my feeling is Shara flew out here a few hours ago. If he really does just want to befriend her, then she's settling in. And even if he doesn't, he'll give her a little time to adjust before making his pitch, whatever that is. Don't you think?"

"You're right on, as always."

"I don't suppose Justin Davis is listed in any of the phone directories?" Max asked.

"Are you kidding?" Jake scoffed. "I'm sure he has a burner phone or two."

"A burner phone?" Amanda asked.

"One of those throw-aways with no contract. You use the minutes, then you're done."

"So they can't be traced," Amanda mused.

"Exactly. But there *are* other ways. My guess is he has a vehicle. There are many ways to go about that search. You said the Thaddeus couple have a police friend who's looking into this for them?"

"We do," Max assured him.

"Call him. Give him the guy's name and he'll contact someone in the Albuquerque PD and they can work together on this. Once we get an address, we'll figure out our next move. Gillian, what are you up to next?"

"I have a feeling, and I don't know why, but I'm going to visit some of the bead and natural stone stores in the morning."

"I've known you long enough to trust your instincts. I'll focus on what I can do. You follow your trail."

"And what are we supposed to do, twiddle our thumbs?" Max asked.

His question didn't daunt Jake. "Go along with Gillian. You can give her valuable information even if you don't think you can. Our finding Shara is a two-way street. There really is nothing more we can do tonight unless you want to go out and search the city, and I don't advise that. I know you're scared and worried, but scared and worried shouldn't add up to stupid."

Amanda saw Max grimace, and she knew Jake had hit a nerve. "Thank you, Mr. Donovan, " she said, "We appreciate all you're doing."

"Call me Jake. We're all going to be on a first-name basis until this is over. Keep in touch," he said, and then he ended the call.

"Jake doesn't waste time," Gillian said with a lift of her shoulder. "He can be excruciatingly blunt, but he's usually right. He has children, so he knows what it is to care about them."

"So there really isn't anything else we can do tonight?" Max asked.

"Make your call to your friend in the police department, and then get some rest. Many of these shops open by nine a.m. so we can be on the road at eight thirty. We're going to discreetly show Shara's picture around. We don't want to alert this Justin that we're onto him."

"In other words, you're warning me not to stand on street corners, show the picture of Shara, and ask where my granddaughter is?"

"Exactly."

Apparently Max could see the sense of what Gillian was saying. He nodded. "I'm going to make that call." He went into the bedroom and shut the door.

"I'm sorry," Amanda said to Gillian.

"No apology is necessary. Everyone's under a lot of strain, and I know your husband doesn't trust what I do. I couldn't help you before. He doesn't think I can help you now."

Amanda gave a resigned sigh. "Thank you for understanding." Amanda had just closed the door on Gillian when her cell phone beeped. She ran to her purse and pulled it free. Checking the Caller ID, she saw the name Grove. Detective Grove. It was late back in Pennsylvania. Why would he be calling now?

"Hello?"

"Mrs. Thaddeus?"

"Yes."

"I tried to call your husband's number but his cell went to voice-mail and he didn't answer at his apartment."

"He's not at home. We're both in Albuquerque, New Mexico. Clare's daughter ran away and we've come out here to find her."

Grove let out a low whistle. "When it rains it pours. Then you're going to have to tell me what you want me to do about this."

"About what?"

"The woman we found that we think could be Lynn Thaddeus. I convinced her to drive up here tomorrow to meet with you, but you're not even in Pennsylvania. What would you like me to do?"

The long search for Lynnie could be coming to an end? But if she and Max dropped the search for Shara, would they lose Clare? What if this woman wasn't Lynnie? What if they never found her?

"Detective Grove, I'm going to have to talk to my husband and to Clare, but I'm thinking if Clare is willing, maybe she can meet with her. Would that be acceptable?"

"Absolutely. Clare's reaction counts as well as yours. The DNA you supplied last week has already been sent to a private lab. I'll send Amy's samples there, too."

"Amy?"

"That's her name now. This woman who could be your daughter."

Amy.

Amanda let the name roll on her tongue, knowing it didn't feel right. But then nothing would feel right until she had Lynnie in her arms once more and Shara back at home with Clare.

Chapter Eight

Shara was scared. Not fear for her life scared, but coming to a strange place, not knowing anybody, not knowing Justin all that well scared. She'd never done anything before like the stuff she'd done today. Using her mom's credit card, she'd accomplished finding a car service online. She'd been chauffeured to BWI. No one had asked any questions about why they were picking her up at the mall. She'd also made her airline reservations online and again no one had asked any questions. After all, she had a driver's license for ID.

Justin was older than she thought. He must be in his twenties, rather than his late teens. With his computer set up in the living room of his three-bedroom ranch house, he was a bit geekier than she expected, too. But he'd shown up at the airport in his truck to meet her. He'd even stopped and gotten her something to eat and told her she could crash with a couple of the girls who worked for him.

She didn't know what work they did for him, but she was sure she was going to find out. One of them—

Courtney—had stopped in to meet her. She'd worn tons of Native American jewelry. Shara loved jewelry, and when she'd commented on it, Courtney said she'd made some of it herself. If Shara was interested in making jewelry, she could drive her to one of the bead shops where she shopped and Shara could get her bearings in the city.

Courtney and Justin had exchanged a look. Justin had smiled and said that was great with him. He had some business to attend to. They could all meet here afterward. So here they were. Courtney had gone to the bathroom to freshen up. From the looks Courtney gave Justin, Shara suspected they were involved. If not, she guessed Courtney wanted to be.

Justin motioned Shara to the sofa. "We need to have a talk about what you're going to do while you're here."

She wasn't sure what he meant, but there was nothing threatening about him. His longish, dark brown hair fell around his face as if he didn't care about style. His rectangular-shaped wire-rimmed glasses sat high on his nose. He was lanky and tall, but in no way foreboding. She'd liked his e-mails and so far, she liked him. Oh, not in that girl-boy way she'd liked Brad, but enough to know he could be her friend. That's what he'd been so far.

"So Courtney took you to her favorite bead shop?"

"Yeah, it was called Zuni. I've never seen so many beads and semi-precious stones. They even had Sleeping Beauty turquoise. The sales clerk showed it to me. She let me slide the beads through my hands. I can never pay for anything like that, but maybe sometime I could afford some of the lapis and the jasper. Courtney says she uses it all the time. I just love her stuff."

"Courtney's good at everything she does."

Justin's smile almost confirmed the fact that he and Courtney had a thing going on. After all, she was blonde with green eyes and a great bod. She'd always wanted to be a blond herself. Maybe she could try that. Out here, she could try anything.

One of the computers sounded a signal and Shara glanced toward it. But Justin didn't get up or go to it to satisfy whatever the little bell signified.

She asked, "What do you do with these?"

"I'm an entrepreneur. If you meant what you said about your family, about your mom and your need to get away, if you'd like to start a new life, I can possibly help you with that."

Up to now, she'd been involved in the excitement of leaving her hometown, of flying for the first time, of noticing everything she could about Albuquerque and the landscape and the beautiful mountains she and Courtney had driven toward when they'd gone to the bead shop. But now she had to face why she'd run away.

"I have to decide what I'm going to do…about the baby." She'd told Justin about that news when he'd picked her up at the airport. He hadn't seemed shocked.

"I know. We'll have to talk about your options."

"But I'm underage. If I go anywhere, wouldn't a doctor notify my mom?"

His eyes narrowed a bit as he studied her. "Not in New Mexico. If you want, though, we can fudge your age, or I can get you a new ID if you really don't want your family to find you."

"A new ID?"

"Sure. I know somebody who can give you a whole new name if you want it, but that's, of course, up to you. You're in charge, Shara. You make all the decisions."

His voice and his promise made her feel less uneasy about the decision she'd made to leave York.

"I want to give you a few things to think about tonight, okay?"

"Sure."

"First of all, you don't have to worry about a roof over your head or food in your stomach. If you work for me, I'll take care of you. I take care of all the girls who do."

There was that phrase again—work for him. "Doing data entry? Something like that?"

Justin dipped his hand into his pocket and pulled out a cell phone. He held it out to her. "This is yours. My number and Courtney's are programmed in. You can call me whenever you need me. Courtney, too. For now you'll be living where she does, so that's probably not going to be necessary. Still, I know how girls like to talk, even if you're only a block apart."

After he handed her the phone, he said, "Let's talk about your baby for a minute, then we'll move on to business."

She hadn't even started to think about her baby. She was still in shock that she was pregnant. But Justin seemed to be the kind of guy who liked to cover all the bases. That made her feel even a little more secure.

"I don't know what I want to do. I don't know if I should have it, or—"

"Your life's in a shambles and this is a lot to think about right now. I'll stand by you whatever decision you make. If you want to have an abortion, I'll pay for it."

"I don't have insurance or anything. I'm on my mom's policy and if I'm out here—"

"Not a problem, Shara."

She could ask why it wasn't a problem, how he could get fake ID's, why he would pay for everything for her, but she was overwhelmed right now. She just wanted to know she'd be okay.

"I realize thinking about the baby is upsetting you, so let's talk about you making some money, okay?"

"By making jewelry like Courtney? She told me she sells it at the flea market."

He gave a low chuckle. "No, I'm not thinking about the flea market. That's something Courtney does to entertain herself. What I'm talking about..." He waved at the two desktop computers. "...has to do with the tech age, social media, and the Internet."

"So is it data entry?"

Again he gave that low chuckle. "Well, in a way I suppose you could say that. But no, we're not dealing with numbers and letters. We're dealing with you and Courtney and some other young women who have decided to make some money in a short amount of time, who need more than minimum wage to live on, who are trying to start over for whatever reason."

"They're not all pregnant!" A terrible foreboding came over her until he gave his answer.

"Oh, no. In fact, you're the only one who's pregnant right now, though Mary Lee did give up a baby for adoption last year. That's one of your options, too."

Since she didn't want to think about that, she still focused on the work. "But what would I be doing?"

Justin stood and went over to one of the computer monitors. With the mouse, he flicked off the screen saver on both of them. Then he jabbed a couple of buttons. He stood in front of one monitor and his visage showed up on the other.

He turned to face her. "Do you understand webcams?"

"My desktop didn't have one. But I was at a friend's when she used Skype so I know how that works." She didn't want him to think she was stupid.

"Yep, you can videoconference with Skype. But I'm talking about a different type of service. I have a website set up and provide a *private* service."

She was getting goose pimples on her arms. "What kind of service?"

"You are a beautiful young woman, so is Courtney, so are the other girls that live in the apartment with her. They each have their own computer with a webcam and their own room for a reason. When they're working they need privacy."

Now those goose pimples ran up her spine, too. "Privacy for what?"

"We have visitors who come to that website who pay a fee to belong. When they check in, they sign up for an appointment time. The broadcasts are live and the girls rotate."

"Rotate talking to them?" she asked lightly, though the feeling in the pit of her stomach told her that wasn't so.

He didn't laugh this time, but he looked very serious. "Talking can be part of it, but their session runs only twenty minutes. You have to think of this more as a lap dance, only there's no danger to you because this person might be on the other side of the world. You'd wear something fairly skimpy like you wore in that photo on *Branches,* and you'd entertain the customer. The girls have lots of books and videos that will help give you ideas on what you can do."

Now Shara *was* scared. Having sex with Brad was one thing, doing something like this for a complete stranger was something else.

"There's total anonymity," Justin explained. "And you won't be seeing the customer. He or she would just be seeing you."

"But I'm pregnant. In a few months I'll show."

"Believe it or not, there are customers for pregnant women. You could be in very high demand. That's something you might want to consider with all the rest. Albuquerque isn't our only location for this. I have another setup in Wyoming and one in Arizona, and I want you to think about what you'll be getting out of this, Shara. You'll have a great apartment with friends. These girls have boyfriends, too. They have a real life. If you want to make jewelry, you can do that. If you want to keep your baby, we can figure something out."

Shara remembered all the Sundays she went to church with her mother and grandmother, the colleges she had started to look into, the future she thought she'd plan. But she was pregnant, and her mom would hate her because of it. Even if she had an abortion, if she let Justin pay for an abortion, if she just gave this a few months, she could stake herself, get a real job, maybe eventually call home.

An abortion. Could she ever do that?

"Have any of the other girls had abortions?"

"That's confidential information," he said solemnly. "But I will tell you this. If you talk to Courtney, she could counsel you about it. With just four clients a day, you could earn enough to be more than comfortable, even get your own place eventually. What do you think?"

"I like Courtney," she said.

"She *is* a peach. Did she tell you her mom and dad have a farm in Georgia, and she sends money home every month?"

"She told me she was from Georgia, that's all."

"You only spent a couple of hours with her, but Courtney's pretty open about her life. She'll talk to you if you're open with her. Same with me, Shara. Don't be afraid to talk to me."

She *wasn't* afraid to talk to him, but she was afraid of other things. Was she able to do what he wanted? Was she able to come on to a man without ever seeing his face? But maybe that was the beauty of it. Maybe she could just pretend.

"What do you think, Shara? Do you think you'd like to be part of my business?"

Just what choice did she have? None.

"I'd like to give it a try."

Amanda had been talking to Clare for the past half hour, trying to ease her fears on so many levels. Max was listening in on the conversation but not saying anything. He looked as worried as she felt. They were all trying to be strong. They were all scared to death.

"Clare, I know you're worried about Shara," Amanda said, for at least the third time, "But if you see this girl and talk to her, you should get a sense as well as we could of whether or not she's Lynnie. You took care of Lynnie. You talked to her in her own secret language. You told her your secrets. You have to have confidence that you'll recognize that bond."

"What if I don't? What if I say or do the wrong things and she leaves?"

"She's having the DNA sample taken. In a short while we'll have the results. So even if she leaves, we'll know for sure, and we have her address. This isn't a one-time only chance, honey. If your interview doesn't go well with her, we'll have another go-around. So please don't put more pressure on yourself than you have to."

Amanda heard a grunt from Max and finally he spoke. "Clare, we should be there with you. We know that. But we also know that Shara is our main concern right now. We've given up so many years in search of Lynnie and who knows if we'll ever find her. But with Shara, we have a good chance of bringing her home. So just keep that in your head when you're talking to this Amy. See if you can get some history out of her. She's probably not going to want to go into any of it if it's bad." He paused. "So just keep in mind that Gillian has a high success rate."

"Dad, I thought you didn't believe in her."

"The truth is, I don't know what I believe any more. But I sure as hell would like to believe in something. If nothing else, I can believe in the skills of Gillian's partner, a private investigator. Tomorrow, you act like an information magnet and collect all you can without sounding like an inquisitor. Listen as much as you can if she'll talk. Do you have one of those little tape recorders with the voice control?"

"I can get one."

"Just turn it on and tape some of the conversation. That way we can listen to it afterward. You'll be fine. I know you will. Did you say Joe's there with you?"

"Yes," she said hesitantly, probably expecting some kind of censure from that.

Max didn't scold or judge. He simply said, "Put your heads together. At least then you'll feel you're prepared."

"Thanks, Dad. That helps."

Amanda saw the grim line of Max's mouth and didn't know what that meant. She took the phone back again and after a few more minutes of conversation, she ended the call. She tried staying calm during it. She really tried to stay calm through this whole trip. But so much was happening and there was so much they didn't know. And tomorrow...tomorrow could be the start of a new life for all of them...or tomorrow could be an ending.

All of a sudden she felt as if the weight she was carrying was way too heavy. All of a sudden, she felt more alone than she ever had in her life. She was sitting on the bed. She shifted toward the wall so Max couldn't see her face, but for once he didn't avoid what he didn't want to see. For once he seemed to realize exactly how she felt.

He sat down beside her on the bed. "Clare will do a good job," he reassured her.

Tears pooled in her eyes and she fought to keep them back. She bowed her head and let her hair flow forward so he wouldn't see.

When Max placed his hand on her shoulder, she thought she'd come apart. The tears just kept coming and she couldn't hide them any more. How many nights had she cried when he'd left to search? How many nights had she cried while he made call after call to police department after police department. How many nights had she cried and lain alone while he'd gone for long drives, taken long walks, been any place but with her.

The ironic thing was, that touch of his hand on her shoulder brought back all other kinds of memories too, from the first touch of his hand on hers at the barn, to their first kiss, to the first time they'd made love. And there'd been no question that it was love. But that was before. This was after. She couldn't let herself feel any of that, not and stay sane for the rest of this. She slid away and his hand fell, but then she cried even harder, and she couldn't keep the sound of her sobs from becoming great hiccups. Max moved even closer and now his arm came around her shoulders.

"Mandy."

When was the last time he'd called her that? When was the last time she'd heard that tenderness? Over twenty-seven years ago?

"I'm sorry. I'm worried about Clare. I'm worried about Shara. I just can't get a grip right now."

There was only a slight hesitation until he brought her into his chest and held her close. He stroked her hair, said nothing, was just Max. She remembered his male scent she'd always loved, mixed with spicy aftershave. She could feel the heat that always seemed to emanate from Max, even in the cold. When the girls were young and they'd go outside to play in the snow, she and Max would sometimes join them. After coming back in, she'd feel like an icicle, but he'd always been warm underneath his flannel and jeans. Her cold feet on his shins always made him laugh. Now his heat seemed to becoming her heat.

The room which had been comfortably air conditioned seemed to be getting warmer, and Amanda realized comfort came in many packages. His comfort was a gift that was fast becoming something else...something she didn't want to feel but that she couldn't turn away from, either. Max's heat as well as his caring was like a powerful web. The temptation to actually be this close to him outweighed her good resolve that she should pull away. She wasn't going to look up at him. She simply wasn't. She was afraid to discover whatever she might find in his eyes.

In the past, there had been so much there— resentment, coldness, a determination that cut him loose. But Max wasn't going to let her hide from him this time. Yes, she had faded into the past and lived for the antique shop, falling on the good times, trying to forget the heartache. But now he was bringing her into the present with him by lifting her chin, shifting toward her, making sure their eyes met. When he dipped his lips toward hers, she froze. She didn't know what to do. They were divorced. They lived separate lives. At one time, they'd probably even hated each other.

At one time, they'd loved each other.

Max's gaze was questioning and maybe even doubtful. In spite of that, he kissed her.

The kiss was familiar yet new. It took her back and it took her forward. It laid out everything he wanted, but questioned everything they'd been. What was she supposed to—

As he angled their heads so he could take the kiss deeper, as he laid her back on the bed and joined her there, she looked up at him and shook her head. "What are we doing?"

"Damn if I know. But I'd just like something to feel good and right for a change. This does."

Were they good together? Were they right for each other? Could they make a new start after everything that had happened?

"What do you want, Max?" she asked softly.

"I want *you*. We need each other right now, Amanda. Let's take what we need and forget the rest."

That wasn't Max's philosophy. He was never impulsive, never reckless. Plan A always led to Plan B, except when he was drinking. But he hadn't been drinking today, or tonight, and he looked as serious as she'd ever seen him.

"What if we regret this?"

"I'd prefer *this* regret to a ton of others, wouldn't you?"

She did want his arms around her. She did want his body joined with hers. She wanted to feel that rush of passion again. She wanted to feel again. His hand went to the buttons on her blouse. Her hand went to the belt of his jeans. Would they regret tonight?

Maybe so, but she'd have even more regrets if she didn't take this opportunity to know Max again...to feel Max again...to love Max again.

Chapter Nine

Clare stood at the hotel room door, not sure what she was supposed to be feeling...or thinking. The sister she hadn't seen for twenty-seven years could be behind that door...or not. Detective Grove had asked her if she wanted him to go with her. She'd said, "No." In a way she was even glad her parents weren't here. They would have muddied up the waters even more.

The thing was—in a way, her mom and dad were leaving this up to her. And what if she screwed it up? What if Amy was her sister and she didn't like Clare? *Enough*, she scolded herself. *Just do it.*

Clare heard the slide of the deadbolt and chain. A precaution anyone would take? Or was it super important to someone like Amy?

The girl—woman rather—who opened that motel room door could have been anyone Clare passed on the street.

Amy Fields had brown with blond highlights. Lynnie's had been golden brown. She had big brown eyes and Lynnie's had been brown, too. But past that...

What had Clare hoped for—instant recognition?

She forced herself to smile. She forced herself to extend her hand and say, "I'm Clare Thaddeus."

Amy was dressed up in Clare's estimation in a pretty lilac two-piece pantsuit. Still so worried about Shara, not knowing what was going to happen next, Clare hadn't thought much about her appearance as she'd grabbed a pair of good jeans and a blue-and-red plaid blouse. She'd tucked it in and worn a belt, but dressing up hadn't gone farther than that. She didn't think she'd slept at all last night. Joe had stayed late, just sitting beside her on the sofa, reaching over to hold her hand now and then. It had been nice. So nice her feelings when he was around worried her, too. She had no business leaning into him...no business depending on him...no business thinking the thoughts she had whenever he was close. Not with her life in the wringer.

Amy seemed to force a shaky smile, too, as if she didn't know what to say or do. That was something they had in common. Amy motioned to the table in front of the window with chairs on either side of it. "I brewed a pot of coffee. Want some?"

Like she needed more caffeine. But with a cup of coffee in her hands, she would have something to do...something to taste...something to focus on. How honest could she be with this woman she didn't know...with this woman who might be her sister? If only the psychic who was helping her parents now could have helped them before. If only *any* psychic had been able to help them.

Clare didn't know what she thought about that. She just knew she had to find Shara and bring her home. She just knew she couldn't lose another person she loved.

Clare slipped a tape recorder out of her purse. "My parents asked me to record our conversation, if you don't mind. Is that okay with you?"

Doubts seemed to flit over Amy's face. But then she nodded. "It's okay. I understand. Detective Grove told me why they can't be here. I'm sorry your daughter ran away."

Clare swallowed hard, knowing she had to get on with this. She switched on the recorder.

"So you drove here yourself?" she asked, still unclear about some details.

"I did. My parents..." Amy hesitated, then went on. "My adoptive parents wanted to come, too. But I needed to come here fresh without my present life weighing me down. Do you know what I mean?"

Clare sort of got that. "You were afraid you might not remember as well if you had your parents' feelings to content with?"

"Exactly."

"So did driving here...being here...wake up any memories?"

Amy looked disappointed when she said, "No. None. Not a hint of anything. Before I left, I talked to my counselor. I've had one ever since my parents adopted me. She said not to expect anything....just to come into the situation and experience it."

"You said you've been seeing a counselor since you've been adopted. Can I ask why? Was it because of the adoption or more? I'm sorry if I have to ask tough questions, but that's what I'm here to do."

Amy shrugged as if this wasn't the most difficult thing she'd had to do...as if this was a conversation with simply...anyone. "I know that. And I thought this whole thing would affect me more. But it isn't. In some ways, I feel like an observer...just hearing about somebody else. If I'm Lynnie, I have no inkling of her. I have no memory of what happened before I was adopted. I didn't even *know* I was kidnapped. And I don't have any memories of abuse...if it happened to me. The doctors think it did. There were signs."

Clare poured powdered cream into her coffee, added a packet of sugar and took a breath. Unbidden memories of her and her sister replayed as if they'd happened yesterday—she and Lynnie playing on swings in the park, she and Lynnie playing tag in the yard, she and Lynnie sitting on the beach. The summer they'd moved into the big house in Pine Hill, her dad had driven them to the beach for an overnight getaway. Lynnie had been afraid of the waves at first. But she'd finally giggled when the water crept up and tickled her toes. She and Lynnie had built sand castles. And she'd whispered to Lynnie that she wanted to stay at the beach forever.

Forever.

She studied Amy and said, "I'm so sorry for whatever happened to you. I was the big sister. I was supposed to watch out for you. I was supposed to keep you safe."

Amy shook her head and her voice was a bit distant as she advised, "Don't do that to yourself. I've had enough counseling to know there's no point to it. Your guilt doesn't affect me. Your guilt won't help me and it certainly won't help you. Whatever happened, happened, and it's done. Done, Clare."

Amy's conclusion made Clare a bit angry. Losing Lynnie would never be done. Not for her parents and not for her. Couldn't Amy see that?

But Amy's traumatic amnesia...or whatever it was...had blanked out the bad.

Amy must have suspected some of what Clare was feeling because she added, "When I was little, after my parents adopted me, I did have some nightmares. There was a monster with a beard. But it was just a shadowy figure. The more my adopted parents loved me, the more those vague visions faded. They altogether disappeared. I've had a happy life with wonderful parents. And I know your life has been affected terribly by what happened, but I can't take that on as my burden."

Sitting back in her chair, Clare just stared at Amy. She couldn't take it on as her burden? How righteous that sounded! How arrogant. How true. They sounded like words coming from a counselor. And maybe all that counseling had become Amy's own. This meeting wasn't anything like Clare expected. Had she thought when she saw her sister again, she'd automatically know her? Talking to this woman was like talking to a stranger.

An understanding of what was happening dawned on Clare like a heavy weight. At this moment, she realized something her parents were going to have to realize, too. Whether this Amy was or wasn't her sister, they'd lost Lynnie...forever.

The Zuni Natural Gem Shop was fascinating. Like any woman, Amanda appreciated pretty things, especially natural stones and gems. From turquoise to agate to jasper, to garnet and amethyst, this shop had it all. She and Gillian and Max stepped inside not knowing what to expect. But what they found were glass cases filled with anything a jewelry maker—from the amateur to the professional—might desire. They were early, arriving just before the shop first opened at eleven a.m. They had been to two other shops without any success, but the name of this one encouraged Amanda to be hopeful.

There was a blonde behind the counter. Amanda surmised she was around college age. Her hair was long and straight, her earrings double-beaded hoops that dangled. She wore a ring on every finger and her nose was pierced. Amanda smiled at her after they entered and the buzzer sounded. She imagined the security on this place was state of the art.

Amanda and Gillian started ooh-ing and aah-ing over the beads in the cases while Max wandered about. As in the other two stores, they had decided to play this casually. Amanda knew Max was restraining himself. He had a tendency to come on too strong and was holding back now so whoever they approached wouldn't clam up.

After Gillian asked to see a strand of picture jasper, the clerk, who had a name tag that said Ruby, unlocked the case and took out the string with its varied shades of brown and rust, gold and black.

"These stones would make a beautiful necklace," Gillian said.

"Yes, they would. A necklace of those would go with most anything casual." She smiled at the clerk. "Do you make jewelry?"

"No, I just wear it," she responded with a small laugh.

"I'm thinking about buying some special beads for my granddaughter. She might have been in recently." Amanda took out her phone and, like a proud grandmother, showed the clerk the picture. "That's Shara. Isn't she gorgeous? She loves turquoise and loves to make jewelry. So I thought I'd find her something nice for her birthday."

Amanda watched for recognition in the clerk's eyes...and she saw it!

"She was in here yesterday," Ruby offered. "I worked the afternoon-to-evening shift. She didn't buy anything, but her friend did. She's in here a lot because she sells her stuff."

"You know, Shara's told me about her." Knowing a little about jewelry-making from clients who came into *Yesteryear*, she adlibbed, "I think she sells at the flea market and craft fairs."

Ruby pointed to a wall where about fifty business cards were pinned. "Courtney's card is up there with her cell number. She takes orders, too."

As if the information didn't matter at all, Amanda strolled over to the board. Her gaze scanned the cards until they fell on the one—the only one—with the first name of Courtney. "I'll add her number to my contact list in my phone and then I'll have it." Amanda did it quickly. Then she suddenly felt a presence by her side.

Max leaned close to her. "You're doing a great job."

"So are you," she murmured back. "Low key isn't usually your bag."

"You were right about how to play this. Let's see what else we can find out." Max dropped his arm around Amanda's shoulders and walked her back to the case. "So take your pick. Buy something for yourself and Shara...and Clare, too. Clare's our daughter," he said with a benign smile for Ruby.

"They're lucky to have parents and grandparents like you. Mine wouldn't think of buying me something like this."

Gillian made small talk with Ruby about her bracelets and rings while Amanda studied the case. She chose a strand of green turquoise in oblong shapes, along with a string of corral. In another case she found a strand of amethyst while Gillian selected rose quartz.

Max looked on as if he was interested...as if he cared, saying off-handedly, "Shara just met Courtney not so long ago. She said something about going over to her place today. Do you know if she lives around here?"

Ruby suddenly looked at Max differently. "Why would you want to know that?"

He shrugged. "You know how it is with kids running in crowds. We try to keep a close eye on Shara. We want to make sure her friends are good for her."

The wariness left Ruby's eyes. "Now you do sound like my parents. I don't know Courtney well. She just comes in here a lot. She's real nice. Buys a lot of silver, too." Ruby pointed to the sterling beads in cases along the back of the store.

"I really should get some of those, too, honey," Amanda said.

Max groaned. "I shouldn't have brought it up!"

Ruby laughed, then she looked up at Max. "Courtney lives with a couple of girls. They're all older than your granddaughter."

He nodded seriously. "Yeah, I'm a little concerned about that."

Amanda admired the way her ex-husband was playing this. He was showing more finesse now than he ever had. She was so proud of him she could burst.

Their gazes met and she remembered explicitly how they'd made love...how they'd fallen back in time...how their attraction had seemed new again.

Fifteen minutes later, they'd taken their purchases and investment in information and returned to the SUV. Once inside the vehicle, Gillian said to Amanda, "Give me the number. I'll text it to Jake and he can see what he can find out. Why don't we have some lunch. I know you two probably don't want to eat, but we don't know what's going to happen next, and it's best to be fortified for whatever comes. Did you think about what you're going to do if you find Shara and she doesn't want to go home with you?"

"We'll convince her that she has to." His voice was determined and Amanda had the feeling that he'd pick up Shara and kidnap her if he needed to. Max wouldn't let anything bad happen to his granddaughter if he could help it.

A half hour later, Amanda sat staring at her food at a deli near Old Town. They'd come to this part of Albuquerque thinking they could walk around while Jake investigated...while Amanda waited for Clare's phone call after her meeting with...Amy. Waiting. It seemed as if Amanda had spent her whole life waiting.

She was trying to chew a slice of pickle when her cell phone beeped. Max's gaze was filled with the same anxiety she was feeling as she fished the phone out of her purse and switched it on. She couldn't put it on SPEAKER in here, so she just answered the call. "How did it go?"

"You have to talk to her, Mom. I can't do this by myself."

Clare sounded so upset as if there were a multitude of reasons why. "Tell me what happened. Is she there with you now?"

"Oh, no. I left because... I left because— Mom, you and Dad have to talk to her. She said she was staying the night yet and that was it. Let me give you her room number."

Amanda found a small notebook she kept in her purse and Max handed her a pen as if he knew what she needed. Maybe he'd always known what she'd needed but just didn't understand how to give it. She jotted down the information Clare gave her. Her daughter's voice was less shaky now.

"What about Shara?" Clare asked. "Have you found her?"

There was desperate hope in her voice and Amanda knew that quality all too well. "We found someone who's seen her in a bead shop. We have the cell number of the woman she's with, and Gillian's partner is getting an address so we have somewhere to go to.

"I should fly out there."

"No, Clare. Listen to me. We don't know what Shara is into, and we're afraid it's nothing good. There's no point that you're in danger, too. Just stay there and wait."

"But she's my daughter."

"I know."

Silence on the other end told Amanda that Clare was thinking about all the times when all they could to was wait...all the times this heartache had plagued her parents, never leaving them for a minute.

"Tell me more about your visit with Amy."

"It wasn't a visit. She's so...removed. She's had tons of counseling and it shows. Not that that isn't a good thing. But I didn't feel any connection. I couldn't tell if she was Lynnie. And, if she is— I'm not sure she wants anything to do with us. I'm so sorry."

"You have nothing to be sorry about. I mean it, Clare. When Dad and I get back to the hotel, we'll call her. I don't think it's a good idea to do it when we're out and about."

"You'll let me know if you find out anything about Shara?"

"If we find out anything, I promise I'll call. We love you, Clare." Amanda felt her voice closing as she ended the call. "You heard my side of that," she said to Max. Her words trembled as she explained that Clare had felt nothing with Amy. "And it sounds as if Amy felt no bond with her!"

He was silent. Finally he said, "We'll call...Amy...when we get back." He reached across the table and took Amanda's hand. "We'll make things up to Clare. Somehow we will. And if Amy *is* Lynnie, we'll figure out a way to reach her. We have to."

At that moment, Gillian's phone beeped. She snatched it up. "Jake?" After a short back and forth, she looked at Amanda then Max. "I have Courtney's address and Jake is e-mailing her driver's license photo. What do you want to do next?"

Chapter Ten

Nothing ever turned out as you expected it to, did it?

Glancing at the clock on the stove, Clare saw that it was almost four. She'd been scrubbing the kitchen ever since she returned home from the interview with Amy and the phone call to her parents. She had to do something to keep busy or she'd go crazy. She couldn't go back to work. She was afraid she'd make mistakes there. So here she was, pots and pans pulled out of the cupboard as she rearranged them, spices on the counter that she wanted to put in alphabetical order. Drawer liner lay on the counter along with the scissors. She couldn't seem to focus on any one task. If her mom didn't call back soon with news about Shara—

She might not call for a while. Albuquerque was a big place. They were three hours behind there. God knew what was happening. She should be there, shouldn't she? Every thought in her head ran into the next one.

When there was a rap on the kitchen door, she stopped cutting shelf paper. She hurried to the door and flung it open, not knowing what she expected to see, or who she expected to see. Maybe her mind had leapt ahead to when her parents would be there with Shara.

But she found Joe. He took one look at her, then stepped over the threshold with take-out bags filling his arms. "You didn't call so I assumed you hadn't heard anything."

"My parents have picked up leads, but..." Her voice faltered. "They don't know anything for sure."

He set the bags on the table, then turned to face her, his hand on her shoulder. "And how did the interview go?"

"It was upsetting and confusing, for me more than for her."

"You should have called me."

"Why?"

He gave her a long, sober look. "We could talk about it. You can't keep this all bottled up, Clare."

"Joe, I don't know what I'm doing. I can't keep a straight thought in my head. Just look at this kitchen. I'm trying to clean and I can't remember what goes in what cupboard."

He dropped his hand from her shoulder. "I thought we were friends."

She averted her gaze, went to the counter, started putting spices back in the cupboard. "We are."

"Clare, stop and look at me." His voice was coaxing.

She slowly turned to face him. "If you want something from me, Joe, I certainly can't give it. Not now."

"Want something? I don't want anything, except for you to lean on me a little. That's what friends do."

"I was thinking not very nice thoughts today. You want me to share those with you?"

He frowned. "You can share whatever you want. I'm not going to judge—"

"Oh, people always say that. But then the words come out of your mouth and they look shocked, and they *do* judge. How can I expect you to be any different?"

"Who judged you?" he asked, gently.

"You're kidding, right? I was an unwed mother. *Everyone* judged me, from my parents to my teachers to friends and neighbors. And now, now I have a run-away daughter. I know how people will look at me. What did *she* do to make her daughter run away? Why didn't she have better control? Why wasn't she a better parent? That's judging, Joe."

"Do you think I asked any of those questions?"

"You're not a regular guy if you haven't."

His lips twitched up in a wry smile. "I've never thought of myself as a regular guy. I'm just me, Clare. You don't think I made mistakes when I was younger, trusted the wrong people, fell in love with the wrong girl? You act as if those things are crimes. They're part of life experience."

"That's one way of looking at becoming a mother before I was ready. But that's the detached way of looking at it. I lived it. I disappointed my parents. I wasn't everything they thought Lynnie would grow up to be. I didn't protect my sister and I obviously haven't protected my daughter."

He was already shaking his head. "You're too rough on yourself."

"The next thing you're going to say is that you don't think my parents are the type to make me feel inferior, to make me feel as if I could never do anything right, to have expectations I couldn't meet. You're going to say they love me and I should just be grateful for that love."

"*Now* who's judging who? You think you know what *I* think?"

Tears welled up much too quickly. "I don't care what you think. It doesn't matter. All that matters is that I lost my sister, and Amy Fields just doesn't seem to be her. And if she is, then that means I'm not too crazy about who Lynnie is all grown up. I only want my daughter back safe and sound and I don't know what to do to get her here."

"Are you going to push everyone away who wants to care about you until that happens?" His voice had a rougher edge now, and Clare realized this conversation wasn't easy for him, either.

"Letting you in takes my focus away from Shara. Can't you see that?"

"No. What I see is a woman who's afraid. You're afraid your parents are blaming you for this, too, though I don't think they ever blamed you for your sister being kidnapped. You're a woman who's afraid that if Shara *does* come back, or if your parents find her and drag her back, she'll just run away again. You're a woman who's afraid to let a man get too close because if he does, he might leave you like *your* dad did...like Shara's dad did." Joe looked as if he was just as shocked he'd said all that, as she was to hear it.

Her voice shook when she said, "I think you'd better go."

"No, Clare, that's one thing I'm not going to do. I'm not going to leave."

"I don't want you here analyzing me. I don't want you here thinking you know me. I don't want you here—"

"Getting closer to you?" he cut in, approaching her with a determined look in his eyes. "Take a deep breath, Clare. Think about it, then tell me you don't really want me here."

She found herself doing what he said, taking that deep breath, thinking about him standing in her kitchen, acting as if he cared. Tears spilled from her eyes and she crossed her arms around herself as if she could ward off what *he* might be feeling as well as what *she* might be feeling...as if she could ward off anyone getting too close...as if she could ward off him.

But unlike so many others in her life, he didn't turn away. He just kept coming. He took her face between his hands and then he kissed her.

Amanda was scared silly, scared out of her mind, scared for all of them. Max had used the search engine on his phone, found what he was looking for, and insisted they go to a small shop where he bought some equipment. Gillian and Amanda had waited outside and he hadn't explained himself or what he'd bought. But she'd seen the sign in the window that said, *Spy Devices*.

This is for Shara, she kept telling herself.

When Max returned to the SUV, he was matter-of-fact. "I can take you two back to the hotel and I can do this myself."

Amanda and Gillian exchanged a glance. "What are you going to do?" Amanda asked.

When he hesitated, Amanda asked again, "Max? You're not going to cut me out of this. Full disclosure."

After what had happened last night, there could be nothing *but* full disclosure. He seemed to realize that, too, although neither of them knew what making love had meant, or what it would mean to their future.

"I bought a listening device. I can put it on the door and hear what's said inside. We need to figure out if Shara's in any immediate danger."

"But what if someone sees you?" Gillian was remaining silent and calm, though Amanda was getting more anxious by the minute.

"That's why I have to scout around first. Actually, this is a good time of day. Fewer people are around in early afternoon. Like I said, I have to scout it out, and I want to get going. Hotel or with me?"

Amanda immediately turned to Gillian. "I don't want you involved in this. We don't know what's going to happen next. You've already done so much."

After a pensive pause, Gillian said, "Max might need more than one lookout. We'll see what the situation is."

So they did. There were six apartments in the building on two floors. The information Jake had given them told them that Courtney lived on the second floor in 2-C.

Gillian pointed out a silver sporty sedan parked a few cars behind the space where Max had pulled in. "That's Courtney's car. The description and license plate matches what Jake gave me."

So as to not attract attention, Gillian and Amanda stayed in the SUV while Max scouted around. Ten minutes later he was back.

"From what I could tell, I didn't see signs of anyone around in the apartments on Courtney's floor. First floor looks pretty deserted too. There's a balcony in the back and a trellis I can climb on. If I sit low in the corner, grill work will pretty much hide me. I can hunker down a while and just listen to what's going on."

"So you'll need us at the sides to make sure no one comes around the back," Gillian suggested.

"Exactly. There's a tall fence at the back of the property that gives the residence a little privacy. That will work to our benefit. No one across the alley will likely catch sight of me, so all we have to worry about is any foot traffic that will come around back. One of you can stay in the SUV and watch from this side. The other will have to come around back with me."

"I'll do that," Amanda said. "There's no reason for Gillian to stick her neck out more than she has to."

"We all have our cells," Gillian said. "Amanda, you and I will keep ours open. That way we can give each other updates. Do *not* hesitate to let me know if you need me back there."

Minutes later, Max had unwrapped the equipment

and was on his way, Amanda following close behind. As he reached the trellis, she caught his arm. "No heroics."

He gave her a crooked smile. "I'll try to remember that."

But Amanda already knew he was just placating her. He would do whatever he had to do to make sure Shara was safe again. They both would.

Last night in bed, Amanda had realized how fit her husband still was. *Ex*-husband she reminded herself. Ex-husband. Maybe last night had been all about the past instead of the future. Maybe it had seemed so overwhelming because they both had so many regrets. But maybe, just maybe, they were on their way to something new, something unsullied by what had happened to Lynnie. When Amanda talked to Clare, Clare's assessment of the situation had battered her heart. If this girl Amy wasn't Lynnie, she doubted if they'd ever find her. Would she be able to tell anything from a conversation that Clare couldn't? Were sisters even closer than parents and children? Clare and Lynnie had been.

There was so much to think about as she watched Max climb the trellis, hike himself over the balcony and crouch down, all without a sound. He couldn't talk to them on his cell because he didn't want to make any noise at all. So if he heard something important, she didn't know what he'd do. They really hadn't planned this out. They really hadn't considered all of the ramifications.

On the other hand, maybe he'd learn nothing up there. Maybe he'd learn Shara never wanted to come home. Maybe they'd be spinning their wheels until a resident of the apartment came home from work and they'd have to leave or get caught.

An hour passed so slowly. Amanda found herself counting the number of slats in the fence to distract herself further. She imagined the photos she had in an album of Clare and Shara when Shara was a baby—at one, at two, at three. At one point she wanted to text Clare to stay strong, but she couldn't because she didn't want to cut her connection to Gillian.

Shara had to be in that apartment, didn't she? Max wouldn't still be listening if she wasn't, would he? Since her line to Gillian was open, she whispered to her, "Are you okay?"

"I'm fine," she heard back clearly. Gillian could speak as loud as she wanted in the SUV.

"Isn't anyone coming or going out front?" Amanda asked her.

"Across the street. No one in this building. I think Max assessed the situation pretty well, but it is getting later and the longer he's up there, the more chance he has of being discovered."

"He has a mind of his own," Amanda muttered. No, she probably couldn't pull him away from that door if she wanted to. All the inhabitants inside had to do was open their blind and they'd see him out there. Then what? Would Courtney call the police? Or would she call Justin Davis and he'd come running.

Suddenly she saw movement on the balcony. "Gillian, Max just stood up. I don't know if he's just stretching or—"

He didn't signal to her. After a few moments, he threw his leg over the balcony, climbed onto the trellis, and made his way down to the ground again. That's when he beckoned to her. That's when he said, "Go get in the car, Amanda."

But the way his brows were drawn together, the way the lines around his mouth cut deep, the way his jaw was set, she suspected they weren't going to drive back to the hotel.

"Tell me what's going on."

"Get in the car."

"Don't order me! Tell me what you found out."

His frustrated grunt said that he saw her determination, the spirit that had helped her survive through Lynnie's abduction and everything that came after, the perseverance that urged her to go on. "My God, Amanda. She's pregnant! They made an appointment for her at a clinic where she can have an abortion. They're leaving soon and I'm going to grab her. So go get in the car and be ready to tie her down if you have to."

Amanda wanted to move, she really did. There was immediacy in Max's tone and she knew there'd be no room for error. But the idea of Shara being pregnant and having an abortion and taking her against her will froze Amanda to the spot.

"I can do this, Amanda. She's a minor. If I have Clare's permission to keep her safe, that's all I need."

He took her by the shoulders and shook her slightly. "Amanda."

This time it was gentleness in his voice and the concern in his eyes that snapped her out of her panic.

"All right," she murmured, giving him a nod, turning and hurrying to the SUV.

Max was right behind her. He didn't get into the car with her, but tossed the equipment inside.

Amanda quickly explained to Gillian what was happening and that Max was going to try to snag Shara. Gillian moved into the driver's seat without saying a word.

Holding the open back door, Max said, "This shouldn't be that hard. She's with one other girl. They'll have to walk by us to get to her car. Amanda, you stay down so she doesn't see you. I'll alert you when they come out. I'll keep my back turned until Shara's within grabbing distance. She was putting up a good front, but I think she's unsure about everything they're doing for her, including her appointment at this clinic."

"But if she wants this—" Amanda began.

"If she wants it, we'll take care of her when we get home, one way or another. But for now, she can't think straight here. She probably assumes we'll turn against her, that we'll reject her because of what's happened to her."

"But we didn't reject Clare—"

"We weren't a united front either, though. We shouldn't have let her reject our help. My fault, again. I *have* learned a few things, Amanda."

They had all learned too many things to count. How would Clare feel when she learned her daughter was pregnant? Amanda knew how *she'd* felt. She'd felt as if she'd done something terribly wrong, as if she'd failed to teach her daughter everything she should know. Had Shara turned to a boy for the love she hadn't felt her family was giving her? Wasn't that why Clare had gotten pregnant the way she had? History certainly did repeat itself. Somehow they had to break this cycle. Somehow they had to show Shara that she was loved. Amanda knew an abortion was not the way to go. If Shara didn't want the baby, if Clare didn't want the baby, maybe she could raise it.

Oh, Lord, what was she thinking?

She was thinking these were the longest minutes of her life.

Everything that happened next happened so fast, Amanda felt as if she were dreaming it. Only dreams weren't this terrifying. Max stood at the passenger door of the SUV, facing the vehicle, glancing over his shoulder every now and then at the door where Shara and Courtney would emerge.

Amanda was hot, her palms sweaty, yet a cold creep of fear crawled up her back.

Suddenly, Gillian, who was holding Shara's earrings in her hand, said, "They're coming."

Although they hadn't appeared yet, this was the notice Max needed to get ready...the notice they all needed. Amanda didn't question Gillian's statement and neither did Max. She saw him tense, half-turn—

The heavy metal door rattled as it opened. Amanda did not stay down. She couldn't. She caught a glimpse of the girl with blond, curly hair. Courtney. She swung her purse jauntily over her shoulder. Amanda heard her say to Shara, "This will be over before you know it. You'll never have to look back."

But Amanda knew if Shara did this, she'd look

back all of her life. Anything involving a child was never black and white. Anything involving a child affected a person for the rest of their lives.

When Amanda saw Shara, she wanted to run to her, but she knew that would be foolish, at least at first. She had to let Max take the lead this time. She couldn't second-guess him. She also couldn't blame him if this didn't turn out right. They had blamed each other for too much, for too long.

But still she was scared for all of them.

The two girls came down the steps and started strolling down the walk. Amanda waited for Max to time this just right. She supposed he was as impatient as always, impatient to get the job done.

The girls were still ten feet from the SUV when Max moved. He called Shara's name, in two strides got to her and said, "Shara, it's me, Granddad. Come on, you're coming home."

No asking, just telling. That was Max.

Shara's eyes went wide, her mouth rounded, and Amanda didn't know if she was going to run, pull away, or scream.

Courtney moved in to yank on Shara's arm, to pull her back toward the apartment. "You don't want to go back with him. You don't want to go back to the life you had. Justin has plans for you."

Max's voice was as stern as Amanda had ever heard it. "I know what those plans are, Shara, and they're not good. You've got to know it, too. We know you're pregnant and it's okay."

"It's okay?" she repeated.

"Come on, I'll drive you to our hotel. We can talk and call your mom. She's worried sick."

Courtney was still pulling on Shara, twisting her away from Max. But Max wasn't going to let her go. He wrapped his arm around Shara's waist, and she wrapped hers around him. She yanked away from Courtney and pulled free. Amanda's heart beat so fast she couldn't breathe.

Max was leading Shara to the car when the unthinkable happened. Courtney pulled a gun from her purse and yelled, "Stop right there. You can't have her. You can't. Justin will blame me."

But Max wasn't listening. All he wanted to do was protect his granddaughter, and Amanda could see that as plainly as she could see them both. He pushed Shara ahead of him and said, "Run to the car."

As she did, Courtney's gun went off.

There was that moment of stark silence, that moment again when Amanda knew nothing would ever be the same. Max's shirt bloomed red at his shoulder. He grabbed at it but ran after Shara saying, "Get into the car, now. Gillian, take off."

Gillian started the engine as Shara climbed into the front seat. Max climbed in beside Amanda, leaned over on her, and his blood dripped into her hands.

Was she going to lose him, too?

Chapter Eleven

Amanda was still shaking. At the hospital, Max had been whisked away, cleaned up, sutured, and bandaged. Now, however, the police were talking to him. Since Shara was underage, another police officer had questioned her while Amanda sat in. At first her granddaughter had been hesitant to divulge all the details of what had happened. But with Amanda's urging, she had.

In another area, Gillian was questioned, because she'd been considered a witness to the shooting.

Beside Shara now in a waiting room, Amanda closed her eyes to try to calm every quivering nerve. Was Max all right? Really? Her mind skipped to the police and the investigation that would probably ensue. If Justin was arrested for his part in all of it—preying on underage girls—if Courtney went to trial, they all might have to return to Albuquerque.

Studying Shara, Amanda didn't like the pallor on her granddaughter's face or her silence. But then she'd been through an ordeal. They all had.

She covered Shara's hand with hers. "Everything's going to be all right."

So many silent moments ticked by, she didn't know if Shara was going to respond. But eventually, though still staring straight ahead, she asked, "Is it? Granddad got *shot* because of me. *You* almost got shot because of me. What's Mom going to say? She probably hates me."

As soon as they'd reached the hospital, Amanda had called Clare, and Max had called the police. Clare had been flabbergasted by everything that had happened and speechless at the idea that her daughter was pregnant.

"Your mother does *not* hate you," Amanda assured Shara.

"Gram, what am I going to do about the baby?" Shara's voice broke. But she went on shakily. "I let Courtney make me that appointment but I don't think I could have gone through with an abortion. I don't want to be a mom, but this is my…baby."

Although Amanda had been through this situation with Clare and could give Shara advice, right now she didn't feel that was the right thing to do. "You have to talk to your mother."

"She's not going to want to talk to me. I know she's not. I fought with her. I stole money from her. I ran. Now with me being pregnant and all, she's going to think I'm an awful person."

Without hesitating, Amanda wrapped her arm around Shara. "She's your mother. She loves you, even when you make wrong decisions, even when she yells and screams, even when she wants to walk out and so do you. We'll all figure this out together. Maybe you can work at *Yesteryear* to pay her back for what you took. But first you *have* to talk to her. She deserves that, Shara, you know she does."

In a little voice, Shara said, "The police took the phone Justin gave me."

"I have mine." She handed it to her granddaughter. "Call. If you want privacy, I'll stand out in the hall." She wasn't going any farther than that. She wasn't leaving Shara alone for a moment, not until she was back in York with her mother.

Shara could hardly hold her grandmother's phone steady as she punched in her home number. She had to prepare herself for her mom screaming and yelling. She had to prepare herself for being grounded for a year. No, not a year, because she'd have her baby before that.

Her baby.

Her mother picked up on the first ring.

"Mom, is everything okay?" Clare asked, obviously seeing her mother's ID on her phone.

"It's not Gram, Mom. It's me."

Shara heard a male voice in the background ask, "Is everything okay? Do you want me to stay close?"

She recognized that voice. It belonged to Joe Lansing. What was he doing with her mom? Maybe they *both* had secrets that weren't going to stay secrets.

"It's Shara," Clare told him. "I think I'd like a little privacy."

"No problem," the deep voice said, and Shara could

hear the truth in that. He really didn't mind giving her mom privacy.

When her mom gave her attention to the call once more, she started with, "Shara—" But she couldn't seem to find any more words. Finally, she said, "Why don't you tell me what happened...from the very beginning."

That wasn't at all the direction Shara had expected the conversation to take. "You mean, from when I left for Albuquerque?"

"No, that isn't what I mean. Tell me what happened to you over the past few months. Tell me what happened that made you think you had to run away."

"Isn't it obvious why I ran away, Mom? I'm *pregnant*. How was I ever going to tell you that? The same thing happened to you and you hated it. You didn't want me." Blinking fast to stop her tears, she suddenly realized nothing she did could stop them.

"Shara," her mom's voice was vehement, but not scolding. "I was seventeen, only a year older than you. And no, I didn't want to be pregnant. But once I was, I *wanted* you. Maybe it was because my mom and dad divorced. Maybe it was because I had lost my little sister. But I wasn't going to lose *you*. I wanted someone who I could love with no restrictions, no conditions, no prior history. Just you and me, babe."

Had it really been that way? *Had* her mom truly wanted her? "I remember Gram coming over and bringing me dresses, presents for my birthday parties, treats in the summer." She could also remember her mom holding her tight at bedtime, bandaging scrapes, whispering, "I love you."

"Yes, Gram did those things, sometimes against my will. I didn't want her giving you anything I couldn't buy. I wanted to show her we could make it on our own. And we have."

"Have we, Mom? Have we made it on our own, or are we just *alone*? Gram was great today. I wonder if I was around her more, if maybe, I wouldn't get so mad at you."

"You think she'd let you buy clothes that are so short you can't walk in them, tops that are see-through where they shouldn't be see-through?"

Shaking her head even though her mom couldn't see, she was honest. "No, it's nothing like that. She just seems to have a different way of looking at things than we do. She wants me to come help her in the antique shop...to pay you back. Maybe I could keep working there to pay for things I need for the baby. If I don't give it away."

"You aren't thinking of quitting school, are you? You have to graduate. That's the only way you'll make a way for yourself in the world."

"It's going to be hard having a baby and trying to keep up with schoolwork. Even I know that. And I'd need daycare..."

"We'll have to talk more about everything to do with the baby. Tell me about Brad," Clare directed. "Does he know you're pregnant?"

"Oh, he knows, and he doesn't want any part of it. Not any part." Her voice broke again and she knew the tears weren't *just* about that. But a lot of them were.

"You loved him, didn't you?" her mother asked softly.

Shara could tell her mother wasn't making fun. She wasn't making it sound as if this was just something teenagers did and they got over it, and then everything would be wonderful.

"I loved him and he didn't love me. On Monday I told him about the baby and he just walked away. Boys don't have to deal with it. They can go on as if their lives were never changed."

"Responsible boys deal with it. Brad isn't responsible. Tell me why you dated him."

"Mom, you've got eyes. He's hot! Ten other girls in the school would love to date him."

"Why did he pick you?"

"Did you think I wasn't good enough for him, wasn't pretty enough for him?"

"Nothing like that, Shara. But why did he date *you*? Pretty only goes so far."

"He told me at the beginning he dated me because I didn't always say yes. I didn't always do what he wanted. I might follow along for a while but then I did what *I* wanted anyway. Believe it or not, he said he liked that."

"One of the first things we have to do after you get home is talk to Brad and his father."

Shara groaned. "Can't you just talk to his dad?"

"Those days are gone, honey. This isn't my mess, it's yours. You're going to have to grow up in the next few months, whether you want to or not."

Grow up. Just what did that mean?

"What should I do? About the baby?"

"You have to consider that question. We have to consider the question together."

"I think Gram and Granddad might want to be involved, as crazy as that seems," Shara said, wondering if she was just being hopeful instead of facing reality. "What Granddad did today was *crazy*."

"What *you* did was crazy. Tell me how you met Justin."

"I had to tell all this to the police officers."

"I'm sure you did, but I don't want read it in a police report, so tell me. When did you become involved with him?"

This was the beginning. This was possibly what growing up was all about—talking about stuff you didn't want to talk about. "He asked if he could follow my page on *Branches*. He was cute in a geeky kind of way, so I told him yes. The other kids on *Branches*, they say stupid stuff. They say their mom is making something for supper they don't like. Things like that. But Justin…Justin helped me. When I was feeling low, he could always type something in that would lift me up, or post a funny picture. We took it off line at Christmas to talk about our families."

"What was his family like?"

"They live in Wyoming, near Cody. They're pretty strict, and that's why Justin rebelled. He's had a computer business going on of some kind since he was my age."

"Mom said he was twenty-three."

"Yeah, I didn't realize that when I came out here."

"Maybe he didn't want you to realize it." She paused. "Why did you trust him so easily?"

"He told me stories of things he went through, sort of like I was going through."

"Do you know if the stories were true?"

"I know everybody doesn't think they are. I know everybody thinks he was trying to manipulate me in something I didn't want to do. Maybe that was true. But he understood me the way nobody else has understood me for months. Maybe years."

After a beat of silence, her mom assured her, "I want to understand you. Do you think you understand me?"

Just what did understanding her mother mean? Shara thought about it. "You go to work. You're tired when you get home. You don't want more problems when you do. So everything I do seems like a problem and freaks you out."

"Like you coming home from the mall with an outfit I don't like?"

"Exactly."

"Don't you see, honey, I'm afraid if you wear an outfit like the one I wanted you to take back, that you'll attract guys like Justin, who don't have your best interests at heart? Can't you see that?"

"He didn't want to have sex with me, Mom."

"No, from what Gram said, he wanted *other* men to have sex with you. Do you really think the webcam money would have stopped there? Don't you think a man who really liked you might call Justin or might call you and say, 'Can't we spend some time together?' That's the way it works, honey. If that had happened, what would you have done?"

Shara felt tears threatening again. "I don't know what I'm going to do *now.* I don't have much time to make a decision. But I can't take care of a baby on my own. I wouldn't be able to go to school. You have to work. What are we going to do?" she asked in an all-consuming panic.

"Shara, stop. Stop right now and breathe. Come on, and take at least three big breaths. You're panicking. I was panicking. We have to stop that. You don't make good decisions in panic. Once you're home, we'll really figure this out. I promise. And I promise you, I won't bully you into what I want. I'll listen to you."

This whole conversation hadn't been what Shara expected. She'd expected scolding and yelling, and her mom making her feel as if she were a total idiot. But that wasn't what was happening here.

"Where's Gram now?"

"She's out in the hall talking to that lady, Gillian. She's pretty neat. She has a sixth sense or something."

"She must have something special to have found you. I thought I'd lost you. I thought you'd never be coming back."

"Like your little sister," Shara murmured.

"Yes, just like that."

"Was that Joe's voice I heard? Has he been…helping you?"

Clare didn't seem to know how to answer that, but finally she admitted, "He and I have become…friends."

"Friends with benefits?" Shara asked,

"Shara."

"Mom, I'm not going to change that much just because I got pregnant. Are you sure you want me to come home?"

Without an instant of hesitation, her mom assured

her, "I want you to come home. But there are going to be changes...for both of us."

She was trying to read between the lines. Maybe *she* needed to give her mom reassurance, too. "Joe's an okay guy, not bad looking either. I'm not totally closed off to what happens in the rest of the world. I hear the news reports. I see the streams on Twitter. Anybody who served the way he did in Afghanistan, well....they deserve a lot of respect. Besides that, he actually seems nice. You've never dated seriously. You've never had someone in your life like that."

"Maybe I should have. Maybe then everything wouldn't have been so hard for you."

"Or you," Shara insisted.

"We'll work out what's best for you, Shara. We will. I don't want you to be afraid of it. I don't want you to be afraid of your future."

"If we could stop arguing—"

"We can try."

An hour later, Amanda hesitated outside of Max's cubicle, not exactly sure why. Maybe because she didn't know where they stood. Maybe because in that moment when he'd been shot, she'd realized, in a way, her world still revolved around him. Was she hanging onto something she should have let go of a long time ago?

She'd cleaned up the best she could, but she still had blood on her top. Max's blood. He was wearing a maroon and green plaid snap-button shirt that obviously wasn't his. One sleeve was cut off so he could put his bandaged arm through it. When he spotted her in the doorway, there were a few awkward seconds when neither of them said anything.

As she approached him, he shrugged. "A nurse found the shirt in the Lost and Found."

"Plaid becomes you," Amanda quipped, trying to keep the conversation light because she didn't know where else to go with it.

"Maybe in Albuquerque," he muttered. "Where's Shara?"

"She's with Gillian. I don't know how we're ever going to thank her. Anyone else would have left after the police questioned them. But she stuck around in case we needed her...in case Shara needed her."

"I'll be giving a donation to their foundation. As soon as my discharge papers come through, I can leave."

"How's the shoulder?" she asked, knowing what he was going to say.

"It's still numbed up."

"Did they give you any pain medication?"

"Not going to take that."

"You're going to be uncomfortable."

"It won't be the first time."

When their gazes met, he threw his legs over the side of the bed, ready to get up. "Shara and I will have to go down to the police station tomorrow so we can be questioned again."

"That doesn't surprise me."

"They arrested Courtney. I don't know all the details.

I think they have a warrant out on Justin. My guess is, they'll try to round up Courtney's roommates and begin questioning them, too."

"Do you think there'll be a trial?"

"I think there will be plea deals. That's the way the system works now."

And Max would know all about the system. "We still have a phone call to make tonight."

"It's getting late in Pennsylvania," he said, checking his watch.

"Shara had a long conversation with Clare on the phone."

"And?"

"I don't know. Shara was crying when she ended the call. They have a lot to patch up, just like we do with Clare."

Max didn't say anything to that.

"Do you think we should reserve another motel room?" she asked.

Max considered the idea. "We're going to be here another night. You and Shara can have the suite. I can get a single."

A single. Maybe they were going to go back to the way things used to be—separate beds, separate lives, a wall between them neither of them could climb. They both had a lot to think about. Maybe her more so than Max because she wasn't going to let Shara give up her baby for adoption. She'd made that decision already.

Just then, however, a nurse bustled into Max's cubicle, a sheaf of papers in her hand. "You're set to go as soon as we go over the instructions."

Amanda wished she had a set of instructions for what was going to happen when she returned to her life in Pine Hill. More than that, she wished she had a script for this phone call tonight with Amy Fields. *Would* she know her own daughter when she talked to her?

An hour later, in their suite at the hotel, Max felt as if he'd been ripped straight down the middle. It had nothing to do with the pain in his shoulder, though the wound was throbbing and hot and probably wouldn't let him sleep tonight. Not as if he'd get any sleep anyway. They had Amy Fields on the other end of the line while he and Amanda shared the speaker phone. Shara was in the other room, probably listening. They'd reserved another room but decided to make the phone call here. Amanda really didn't want to let Shara out of her sight, and he understood that too well.

"Did you feel anything when you were talking to Clare today?" Amanda asked Amy.

Max didn't roll his eyes as he usually did—at least inwardly—after Amanda asked the question. She was all about feelings. She always had been and always would be. He was about shutting them out while she wanted to let them all in. He'd let a few in last night and he almost regretted that. He'd seen the hope in Amanda's eyes this morning and hadn't known what to do about it. He was used to a life alone now. Wasn't that what was best for him? He still had nights when at midnight, he made a call to his sponsor. He still had days when the best thing he could do was attend a meeting. Amanda didn't know his life now.

He heard Amy say what he knew Amanda wouldn't want to hear. "Clare's very nice, but I didn't feel anything. I just met her. Or at least I think I just met her. Mrs. Thaddeus, you must understand, I live in the present, each and every day."

He saw Amanda wince at the *Mrs. Thaddeus*. If Amy was their daughter—

"Call me Amanda," she swiftly said, though he could hear from the thickness in her voice that she'd been affected by the title. "We know you're driving back to Pittsburgh tomorrow, but Max and I would really like to talk to you once we get back. If you can't come to us, we'll come to you."

"You mean after the DNA results?"

"We don't know exactly when those will be ready, and I'd like to see you, face-to-face."

"When you're back," Amy said reasonably, "then we can decide."

Max cleared his throat. "Amy, we don't want to pressure you into anything, but Amanda and I have been searching for our daughter for twenty-seven years. You might be her. We'd at least like the chance to talk to you in person. We understand we're a disruption in your life, but a face-to-face meeting over coffee shouldn't be too much of a disruption, should it?"

There was silence. Finally, Amy responded, "No, I guess not. You have my cell number. When you get back, call me. And Mr. Thaddeus, I'm glad you found your granddaughter."

They all said their good-byes. Then Max turned off the speaker phone, and the call was over.

Amanda turned away from him and he knew what that meant. She was trying to control her emotions and couldn't. She was afraid to let him see them. Had she always been afraid? Had he always denied them? Last night he hadn't and look what happened. Right now he could do nothing about them because Shara was in the next room.

He didn't put his arms around Amanda, but he did the next best thing. He clasped her shoulder.

She shook her head.

"We'll see her when we get back."

Amanda still didn't turn around. "I couldn't tell. I couldn't tell anything. She was so distant, so removed, and I didn't feel as if I broke through even just a little bit."

Amanda's voice shuddered. His fingers tightened, telling her he understood.

Shara sat on the sofa, glancing at them, obviously not knowing what to do. That was the problem. None of them knew what to do, and hadn't for many, many years. He couldn't tell Amanda everything would be all right. He'd done that at the beginning and he'd been all wrong. He'd been wrong about so many things.

After he released her shoulder, he took action like he always did when he didn't want to face the emotions of the moment, when someone he cared about was hurting. "I'm going to move my things to my room. There's someplace I have to go and I'm going to have my phone turned off for a while."

At those words, Amanda did turn around to face him. There were tears on her cheeks, but she swiped them away and looked at him with huge, questioning eyes that reminded him so much of that day he'd kissed her for the first time.

"Where are you going?" she asked.

"To a meeting."

Chapter Twelve

If Clare thought her troubles would be over once Shara was home, she was sadly mistaken. From the moment Clare met her at the airport and hugged her, Shara had been quiet and brooding. Not hostile, but brooding.

The day after Shara had flown home with her grandparents, Clare had cooked a dinner Shara liked best—roast chicken, mashed potatoes, cauliflower au gratin and even chocolate cake with fluffy white icing. But Shara had just picked at it. Clare didn't know what to do—not about her daughter...or about Joe. She and Shara had just finished dinner when he came to the door.

After a hello and a weak smile, Shara had excused herself and gone to her room.

Joe glanced at the table and the food. "Did I interrupt?"

"No, we were finished. Neither of us was hungry, and neither of us had much to say."

"She has big decisions weighing on her. Maybe you just have to let her think them through."

"And just how much do I influence her, when I don't know what's best for either of us? I made an appointment at the Planned Parenthood Center. She needs to talk to a counselor. Maybe we both do."

He came closer. "What do you really want?"

"I want none of this to have happened," she answered honestly.

He gave her one of those Joe-looks that brought her back to reality, and he kept silent with no judgment and a lot of understanding.

She sighed and picked up the dish of mashed potatoes, carrying it to the counter. "As I said, I don't know what I want. Do I want Shara to have an abortion? No, everything in me screams in protest at that solution. Do I want her to give the baby up for adoption? How would any of us feel knowing that a child who belonged to our family was out there somewhere, and we weren't the ones to protect it, to raise it, to nurture it? Do I want her to keep the baby and learn what's it's like to be a mother at sixteen, to worry about food and shelter and daycare? Do I want to raise this baby and let Shara pretend to be its big sister?"

He was about to wrap his arms around her when she stepped back and wouldn't let him. "Joe," she said in a whisper. "We can't, not with Shara here."

"Clare, really? Come on now. Maybe it would do her a world of good to watch a caring relationship develop."

Clare could see that pulling away from Joe had hurt him and she didn't want to pull away. But what choice did she have? She was about to say *This isn't going to work* when the phone rang.

A sign maybe? A sign that she shouldn't burn this bridge? That she should let Joe into her messed-up family?

Joe was closest to the phone and could see the Caller ID. "Tessa Kahill Winthrop. I think that area code is a Connecticut number."

Tessa Kahill Winthrop. The name sounded familiar but Clare couldn't pinpoint where she'd heard it. "Connecticut?" Not knowing what was going to happen next these days, she held out her hand for the phone.

Joe took it from its base and put it in her hand.

"Hello?"

"Clare Thaddeus?"

The voice was pleasant enough, and again sounded almost recognizable though Clare couldn't figure out why. "This is Clare. If you're selling something—"

"Not exactly," the woman answered. "I'm a journalist and I have a cable news show out of New Haven—NEWS NOW. I used to stick mainly to foreign affairs, but we've broadened the scope of the show."

Tessa Kahill Winthrop. Now Clare recognized the name. When she'd had a sick day or was home on holiday, she often watched Tessa's show and admired her. Before this program, the journalist had done a lot of specials. Clare remembered one in particular. Tessa had interviewed a woman whose sister had gone missing. It had been poignant and in good taste, not at all sensational.

"I'm familiar with your program."

"Well, that's good. At least you know I'm legitimate because I have a feeling you're going to be getting quite a few calls now that the story has broken."

"The story?" Was she talking about Lynnie?

"The story about your daughter, and Justin Davis, and Courtney Waters. It's gone public, or didn't you know."

"No, I didn't know. We're dealing with some things here and…"

Suddenly the doorbell rang. Joe nodded toward the living room. "I'll get it," he said in a low voice.

When Joe opened the door, Clare heard her parents there.

"What do you mean the story's broken?" she asked the journalist.

"It's all over cable news—what the police found, all the computers, the webcams, the ring of girls who are underage and working for Justin Davis."

"Oh, my gosh."

"As I said, you're going to be receiving a lot of calls. I wanted to be one of the first to ask you to tell me your story. You see, I've researched you and your family. I discovered the story about your sister being kidnapped twenty-seven years ago."

"I haven't received any other calls."

"That's because our network is on top of every story that could be a good one. Sorry, I meant in a journalistic sense. Your news story is just hitting social media. And somebody's cell phone video of the shooting in Albuquerque is being uploaded as we speak. In half an hour, everyone will know about Justin Davis's ring. You know how things go these days, right?"

Oh, yes, she did. "So good journalists are going to dig until they eventually go back to my sister's kidnapping. Is that what you're saying?"

"Exactly. We try to make as many connections as we can. Unfortunately, this story has a lot of them."

As well as one Tessa Kahill Winthrop probably didn't even know about—Amy Fields and the DNA results they were waiting for.

"Clare, may I call you Clare?"

"Yes, you can."

If this had been a strange reporter, or a journalist Clare had never heard of, maybe she wouldn't have given her permission. But Tessa was giving her a heads-up and there had to be a reason why.

"Clare, if you've watched my program, you know I delve into women's issues. The interview I want to do with you isn't so much about the shooting, but what happened to your daughter. It's not so much about Justin Davis, as it is about run-aways and what can happen to them. I'd like to think by putting this story out there—your story—we can help some girls...help some young women."

"You realize I can't give you an answer right now. I have to talk to my daughter about this, and to my parents. We're all involved."

"Of course, you are. This is a family story. I definitely want to concentrate on that angle. Maybe it's because I'm pregnant right now—"

"*You're* pregnant?"

Tessa gave a little laugh. "Not showing much yet. Not officially announced. But, yes, I am...and over-the-moon happy about it, too. I might cover foreign affairs, but my family is my world. So let me give you some other numbers where you can reach me besides the one you have on Caller ID. Call me after you've discussed this with your family. I'd like this to happen soon. This week if we can manage it. And Clare, as I've said, if it's possible, I'd like to interview your whole family, not just you and your daughter. But I'll take whoever I can get."

After Clare ended the call and went into the living room, she saw Joe trying to make conversation, her mother trying to oblige, but her father was looking like the last thing he wanted to do was make small talk.

That was a certainty when he said, "We need to prepare you for something, Clare. I got a call from someone in the Albuquerque police department, the detective who handled most of my questioning. There's cell phone footage of the shooting and it's going to go public. They'll blank Shara out, of course, because she's underage, but there's going to be questions and digging by reporters. They're going to find us."

"I know. I just had a phone call from a journalist." She went on to explain about the call, and about what Tessa Kahill Winthrop wanted.

When she was finished, her father shook his head. "She can't expect us to lay our lives out like that. If we get into why Shara ran away, if we get into when Lynnie was taken, my God, there's the divorce and Amy Fields appearing. I won't be a part of any interview that does that."

"Dad, did you listen to me? This is about helping other girls. The focus will be on Shara and why she ran away, and what almost happened when she did."

"Oh, sure, this reporter says that now," her dad muttered.

"I believe she means it."

"You had one conversation with her, and you think she's going to be honest with you? That's naive Clare."

"And just what would you prefer? You think having reporters dig up all the grimy details themselves will help anybody?"

His brows were furrowed, his eyes stormy. "This is one blip on the news cycle. It will pass quickly if we don't feed it."

But Clare didn't believe that. There was plenty of damage that could be done if her family didn't have input. "Mom, what do you think?"

Her mother had been strangely quiet since her return, too. Very introspective. That scared Clare. Her mom had been detached that way after Lynnie disappeared. But then in the past few years, especially, she'd seemed to find herself again. She'd seemed to find what made her happy.

"I watch Tessa's program almost every day," her mom responded. "Her show carries a lot of weight. I think that's because she's genuinely interested every time she does an interview. She just finished up a series about parents who adopt. It was quite moving."

"So you would want to do this?" Clare asked her mother.

"I would be willing if there was a greater good. Heaven knows some good should come from all this, don't you think?"

Her father was still scowling, and Clare turned to Joe. "What do you think?"

"Are we taking a vote?" her father asked acerbically.

To Clare's surprise, her mother reached over, took

her dad's hand and squeezed it. That was a gesture she *wouldn't* have seen a week ago.

"I don't get a vote, Mr. Thaddeus," Joe responded. "At least not yet." He glanced at Clare, gave her a small smile that made her stomach flip flop, even in spite of the circumstances. Then he went on. "What any of us in this room think doesn't really matter though, does it? Isn't it Shara who's going to have to make this decision?"

Joe was right.

"We can't put this on her shoulders," Amanda said with determination. "She has enough she's thinking about, and that's why we're here tonight. Clare, have you talked about forgetting the idea of an abortion?"

"I made her an appointment at Planned Parenthood."

"To have it done?" Amanda's voice rose and Clare realized her mother was a lot more upset than she was letting on.

"No, for a counseling session. I'm hoping if someone objective talks to her, it will make it easier for her."

"Objective?" her mother protested. "That's the whole point. We don't *want* someone objective. We have to show her the right route to take."

"And how do we know that adoption isn't the right route for her, if not abortion?"

"You can't give my grandchild away. How could you even think about doing that?"

"How can I think about giving a child away? The same way you and Dad practically forgot I existed while you were looking and longing for Lynnie. You want Amy to be the daughter you lost. What happens if she is? Will you forget about me and Shara, and try to make up for all those years you lost? I was a second-class citizen before, and I won't be again. I won't let Shara be."

This time Max took her mother's hand and he squeezed it hard. Then he released it and stood. Crossing to Clare, he did something he hadn't done since she was a little girl. He put his thumb under her chin and tipped it up so her gaze met his.

"Your mom and I are driving to Pittsburgh Monday to meet with Amy. But whatever happens with her, your mother and I know we didn't appreciate you when we had the chance. We're trying to do that now. If we found Lynnie again, if Amy is Lynnie, we wouldn't just have lost years with her to catch up on. We have lost years with *you* to catch up on."

Shara had come out of her room and was standing in the hall listening.

Max motioned her to come closer. "We have a lot to discuss with you, Shara. Come on, sit down and talk with us."

She looked around the room but she didn't move forward. Instead she asked, "Are you going to fight?"

"We won't fight. One thing is clear. We want what's best for you."

Amanda suddenly stood. "I have something to say, and I want all of you to understand I've put a lot of thought into this." She looked straight at her granddaughter. "Shara, if you don't feel you can raise this baby, I understand. Clare, if you don't feel you can raise this baby, I understand. But I think the three of us, together, could. If

I have to close *Yesteryear's Treasures* to be daycare you can trust, I will do that. But more importantly, if neither of you want to raise Shara's baby, I will do that, on my own if I have to. I will not let another child slip away."

Clare knew the stunned expression on her father's face said it all. He never expected that commitment to come out of his ex-wife's mouth, and neither had Clare.

They all talked in circles after that, not really getting anywhere, not until Shara said, "I want to do the interview."

Shara had plopped down on the floor cross-legged while Clare sat on the hassock beside Joe's chair.

"This could be in front of the world, honey," Clare said. "Do you really want to put your life out there like that? Do you want to talk about the past few months? Your relationship with me? What happened with Brad? What happened with Justin? Are you really ready to go public with all that?"

"I don't want another girl like me to run away and think she's okay on her own. I don't want anyone else to think they can meet somebody on line and trust them. If I don't talk about this, who's going to?"

Shara was right about that. "Mom?" Clare asked.

"I want to do the interview with you."

"Dad?" Clare asked.

"Count me out. I don't want to be associated with the shooting. I don't want the notoriety. And I especially don't want the press."

"All right then. It looks as if I'll call Tessa and tell her the three of us are going to do it."

Max stood. "I think we've all had enough of this

for one night. Give it another twenty-four hours," he suggested with a pointed look at Clare and Shara and Amanda. "Make sure it still seems like good sense then."

Up early Monday morning to get the shop in order before she and Max drove to Pittsburgh, Amanda sat at her kitchen table with her laptop, checking her e-mail. She had a hundred things on her mind at least. The discussion at Clare's uppermost. She hadn't changed her mind about any of it—not about adopting the baby, not about doing the interview. Joe would be driving her and Shara and Clare to Connecticut on Wednesday, taping the interview on Thursday, and driving back Friday. An executive for the news program had offered to fly them in or buy their train tickets. But instead of spending time in an airport or taking a train, Joe said he could drive them and they could stop as much or little as they wanted.

She wasn't worried about being away from *Yesteryear*. She'd been on buying trips before, and her assistant and her two clerks had handled her absence just fine. But she *was* worried about Max—what he was thinking and what he was feeling. At least now he told her exactly what he was thinking, but the feeling part—

He didn't want to do this interview because he didn't want to delve into the pain. She couldn't blame him. But Shara and Clare needed this interview. Maybe, so did a million other moms and daughters out there who would watch it. Maybe by doing the interview, all three of them would figure out what was best to do.

After the laptop booted up, her e-mail downloaded. Her heart practically stopped when she studied the address on one of them. Schuster Laboratories. She clicked on it and read it for what it was—a notice that information had been loaded into her account on the Schuster website. She had it bookmarked. All she had to do was sign in with her password and some of the uncertainty of the past twenty-seven years might end.

Her cell phone rang and at first she wasn't going to pick it up from its charging dock on the counter. Maybe to put off the inevitable, she crossed to it and checked the called ID. It was Max.

Maybe he already knew. Maybe he'd already checked his account at the Schuster website.

She picked up the phone. "Do you know?" she asked him.

"I didn't check my account yet. Did you?"

"No."

"I'll be right over. We should do this together."

That thinking was progress, she supposed. They'd done more things together in the past week than they had in the past twenty-seven years. Did he want to do this together for his benefit or for hers? Did it even matter?

He clicked off before she'd say she'd wait. Typical Max.

But she loved the typical Max. She always had and she always would.

Not ten minutes later, he was standing at her door, and she was letting him in. He was dressed in jeans and a white Oxford shirt, open at the neck with the sleeves rolled up. He was as ruggedly appealing as ever and she let that distract her for a moment...just a moment. But then she was turning away from him, going to her laptop, moving her cursor to the bookmark, clicking on the Schuster site.

Max closed the door and came to stand behind her. "We must have been downloading e-mail at the same time," he said.

"We must have," she murmured, typing in her password, entering the portal that could give them gloriously happy news or the limbo they had existed in ever since Lynnie had been taken.

He was crouching down beside her now, studying the document as she opened it. They both read the findings at the same time. They both understood exactly what the document was telling them.

While Amanda took a couple of deep breaths and swallowed hard, Max stood. When she looked up at him, she felt as if all the air had been knocked out of her. He looked as if any hope he'd once held had finally died.

She said it first. "She's not Lynnie."

"No, she's not."

"That's why I didn't feel anything. That's why Clare didn't feel anything. Oh, Max, we're never going to know."

He pulled her up to him then and enfolded her into his arms. "We're never going to know," he agreed, holding onto her tightly, as tightly as he had the night they made love. After a short while, he pulled away from her. "We have to call Amy and tell her we're not coming."

Amanda tried to get hold of herself, tried to push all her dreams away, tried to claim reality and deal with it. "She probably received that e-mail this morning, too."

"I'm sure she did. She's probably happy about it. I don't think she really wanted to know where her parents are. She didn't want the complications of dealing with the past."

"But we still have them. Come with us to New Haven, Max, please."

He shook his head. "No. You do what you have to do."

She swallowed hard again. There would be no changing his mind. He'd always been stubborn. He'd always been decisive. He'd always been Max. He was going to put this episode with Amy Fields behind him and pretend it never happened.

"Why don't I make us some breakfast. I meant what I said about adopting Shara's baby if she and Clare don't want to raise it. We should talk about that."

"Not this morning, Amanda. Not yet. Since we're not driving to Pittsburgh today, I have a pile of work on my desk that I can attend to. Do you want me to call Amy?"

She was hurt at his attitude but she understood why he wanted to shut down, why he wanted to bury himself in work. So she said, "I'll call Amy. Why don't you call Clare."

Max took out the phone, obviously anxious to get

the deed done. He moved to the living room so he could have a private conversation with Clare while she had one with Amy.

Separate rooms...separate lives all over again.

This time, Clare called Joe. No matter that the day had barely begun at eight a.m., no matter she was supposed to be at work in an hour, no matter she should talk to her mother first and tell her how sorry she was. Her father hadn't sounded heartbroken but he *had* sounded resigned. Her mother—she'd be seeing her this evening. They were going to talk about what they needed to take along to Connecticut, what they should wear. This would be Shara's first day back at school and they could talk about how that went, too. There was so much for the three of them to talk about, including Amy Fields.

Joe picked up on the second ring. "Clare?"

His voice held a question, maybe because of the way he'd left the other night. They hadn't finished the conversation they'd started before her parents had arrived. After they'd left, he'd gone, too. He hadn't known where he stood. What with all the turmoil she was in, he'd obviously decided not to press. She'd been grateful for that then. But now?

"Amy isn't my sister. The DNA results came through."

He didn't question her about the results. He didn't ask her what she was feeling. He said simply, "I'll be right over."

She didn't protest this time because she wanted him here beside her.

After Joe opened the door, he took one look at her, folded his arms around her and guided her to the sofa. They sat there in silence until she tucked one leg under her and faced him. "I knew she couldn't be Lynnie. I think I'm more relieved than disappointed because deep down in my soul I knew."

"But your parents are another matter?"

"Mom's probably heartbroken. More than ever, she'll be ready to adopt Shara's baby. She wants to fill that hole that Lynnie left."

She studied Joe's face, the lines around his eyes, the strong jaw, the mouth that had kissed her with promises of a lot more to come if she was willing. "I have to ask you something," she said.

"Ask."

"I need to fill that gaping hole, too. In a way, I have to make our family whole again. The way for me to do that is to raise Shara's baby. For good or bad, right or wrong, I'm going to convince her to have her baby, to let me and Mom help her, to mend the past and look toward the future. I don't know how I'm going to do it, and I suspect all of our lives are going to be a mess for a while."

"You haven't asked me anything yet," he said seriously.

That's because she was afraid. She hadn't asked him because she hadn't taken any risks in a very long time. The question was in her heart. It just wouldn't come out of her mouth. But finally after a deep breath, and a prayer for courage, she asked, "Do you want to get involved with me...with my family, or is all of this just too much to take on?"

His answer was a slow smile. His answer was opening his arms to her. His answer was clear. "I'll take on you and your family, Clare, because I think we can have a good life together. After all, I've always wanted to be a dad...or a grandpa."

Clare wrapped her arms around Joe's neck and kissed him.

Chapter Thirteen

On Wednesday evening at the edge of dusk, Max did something he hadn't done for at least the past five years. He drove to Pine Hill and parked across the street from the house with green siding and black shutters where he and Amanda, Lynnie and Clare had lived. They'd still had boxes to unpack when Lynnie had been stolen. They hadn't really even found their life there yet. He'd moved his family to the suburbs, a small town out of the city because he'd finally been making some decent money, and the price of a house had been more reasonable there. Lynnie and Clare had had their own rooms. There was a guest room, a den for him, a family room besides a living room. Every night Amanda had cooked dinner and he'd tried to get home at a decent hour so they could all sit down together. It had been a stable life, the life he'd envisioned, a good life. He had a wife to love and children to nurture, and more than he'd ever dreamed of.

Now he studied the house whose siding was faded. It would soon need a new roof and the shutters replaced or repainted. He wondered if the inside had been changed drastically.

He also wondered if Clare and Shara and Amanda had gotten settled in their hotel in New Haven. Then he remembered, Joe had driven them. He was looking out for them...looking after them.

Max shifted in his seat feeling uncomfortable with that thought. Uncomfortable...because that was *his* job.

However, he'd abdicated the position of caretaker, provider, protector and defender years ago. When Lynnie had been kidnapped? When he and Amanda divorced? When Clare had gotten pregnant? All life events that had shaken up his world, and Amanda's, too. In some ways, she'd weathered the storms better than he had.

Suddenly the door to the house opened. A couple stepped out who both looked to be about Clare's age. After them, three kids tumbled over the threshold onto the porch. There was a boy about eight, a girl who could have been five or six, and then there was a little one...a little girl who toddled out who couldn't have been more than three. She had pigtails tied with pink ribbons. Amanda used to fix Lynnie's hair that way.

All at once, Max couldn't stop the parade of pictures flashing in his mind, so many pictures that he'd kept tightly locked in an album in his heart—Amanda kneading dough to make sticky buns just like her mother had...Lynnie on a booster seat at the table, mashed potatoes all over her face as she fed herself like the big girl Amanda told her she was...Clare in a pink tutu and ballet shoes practicing for her recital, looking up at him and asking him what he thought of her pirouette. The pictures of Lynnie he'd kept stowed away seemed bigger than life as she wrapped her arms around his neck and gave him a smooch on the cheek...as she held his hand when they crossed the street...as she cuddled against him in a pink flannel nightgown when he'd read her a story.

At first he thought the pain was in his shoulder again. It was still sore and throbbed and gave him fits when he did things he wasn't supposed to do. But the pain wasn't in his shoulder.

It was in his heart. Sitting outside this house, stepping back in time, remembering the family he once had, the little girl he'd once held in his arms, he couldn't keep the pain locked up in a box any more. With the pictures it burst open, practically overwhelming him. As he watched the family climb into their mini-van and drive away, he felt wetness on his hand. When he looked down another drop fell.

He was crying.

Grown men didn't cry.

Strong men didn't cry. That's what his father would have said. But his father had been a drunk and mean and what the hell had he known?

Max couldn't sit there another moment...couldn't remember a perfect life...a destroyed life...a little girl who would never return. He switched on the ignition in spite of his blurred vision. He backhanded his eyes, willing the tears to stop. Feeling like a fool, he drove back to his apartment.

After he parked and let himself inside, he went numb. He wanted a drink so badly his hand shook. The memories could drive him to drink again. He should call his sponsor—

But he knew what the man would tell him. Scott would advise him to *feel*. *Feel* was the last thing he wanted to do.

Yet the photo review in his mind wouldn't quit. He sank down into a recliner he hardly ever used—sitting still was always too dangerous because it provoked introspection he avoided—and let the memories stream like a never-ending movie. The tears burned again. But this time he didn't focus on them...he focused on his wedding day, Clare's birth, Lynnie's baptism. Amanda kept photos of it all and he knew she often sat and cried over them. But he didn't need the albums. All the pictures were in his heart.

He wasn't aware of time as he sank into memories...as he re-experienced love and pain. He'd kept everything bottled up for years because he thought that was what he was supposed to do. But what he was supposed to do had lost him everything...and everyone.

Sitting in the dark, he ran his hand over his face, heaved in a shuddering breath, and knew the life he'd been living had been no life at all. He needed to change that. He needed to wake up before his life was over, even if he never knew what happened to Lynnie. He could still grab some happiness before he lost everything that mattered most.

Since his return from New Mexico, he hadn't been able to forget his night in Albuquerque with Amanda—not the passion, not the fervor, not the pleasure, not the...love. He still knew Amanda well enough to acknowledge the fact that she never would have made love with him again if she didn't still love him.

Maybe the same was true for him.

So now what?

Now he needed some light. He switched on the floor lamp and checked his watch. It was midnight! For hours, he'd been sitting there replaying his life. He had too many regrets. He'd made too many mistakes. The latest? Not accompanying Amanda, Shara and Clare to New Haven and taking part in the interview. He should have gone with them. He shouldn't have fought the idea of talking to the journalist. He should have supported Amanda and Clare and Shara by participating, giving them moral support and jumping into a conversation they should all have.

Hindsight was 20/20, true. But the past could teach if he'd let it.

He loved Amanda and he wanted her back. That he was sure of. He wasn't going to stand by again and watch his future head south.

New Haven was a five-hour drive. He would get to that interview. He would prove to Amanda that he was the man she'd always known he could be.

Amanda was following Tessa, Clare, and Shara down a corridor to the set where they'd be taping their interview when her cell phone vibrated in her pocket. Maybe it was Max, wishing them good luck at least.

But it wasn't Max. It was Gillian. She'd sent a text that said—*I know the taping will go well, and you'll help lots of families. E-mail me and let me know how it goes.*

Amanda had spoken to Gillian last night when Gillian had called to ask about Shara and how she was faring now that she was home. Amanda had filled her in on everything and she suspected that they were going to stay in touch. She hoped so. Gillian was a special person.

They'd almost reached the studio when Amanda heard her name.

"Amanda, wait."

It sounded like Max. It couldn't be Max. He was back in York.

"Amanda," he called again, and then he was there, looking out of breath and harried, his pale blue Oxford shirt looking a bit wrinkled, his old jeans faded from many washings.

"Max, what are you doing here?"

"I thought I'd have plenty of time. I thought I could drive here, see you at the hotel, change clothes—"

"You drove?"

"All night. There was an accident on the Interstate and I got held up more than once. But here I am. I want to do the interview with you. More than that." He took her hands between his and looked deeply into her eyes. "I want to marry you again. I want to become a family again. I love you, Amanda. I always have. I could never admit how much I felt, what I felt, but I am now. You know what I am. I can be a workaholic sometimes. I'm going to have to go to meetings. I might call my sponsor in the middle of the night, but I want to live each day beside you and recreate that night we had in Albuquerque."

"Oh, Max, I've been waiting for you to wake up. I've been waiting for so long… Yes, I'll marry you again. Yes!"

Max took a kiss that was deep and hard but short because he knew others were looking on. When he broke away, Amanda saw Tessa looking as if she'd just found the story of the century. Shara was grinning and Clare was teary-eyed, and Amanda felt like laughing and crying all at the same time.

Max squeezed her close, but then asked the journalist, "Can you pull in an extra chair for this interview?"

She answered him with a knowing look that said she was already rethinking her questions. "I sure can."

In Pittsburgh, Beth sat at the work station in her living room finishing up a website design for her client. She just had a few more bells and whistles she wanted to add. She took a break this time every morning to watch Tessa Kahill Winthrop's program NEWS NOW on one of the cable news channels. The journalist had a way with words and a point of view that Beth liked. She spent most days in her apartment working from eight to five, even though her adoptive parents encouraged her to get out more. But she was a homebody because of her background, a homebody because of her past, a homebody because she had a past and shadows she'd had to overcome in order to have close to a normal life, though who really knew what "normal" was.

Using her remote, she turned on the cable channel and swiveled her chair around for a good view. She was few minutes late turning the program on today, and Tessa was in the middle of her interview.

"So you're ready to raise your daughter's child?" Tessa was asking.

Beth froze. She studied the young woman's face Tessa was addressing. She was practically Beth's mirror image!

She turned up the volume.

"Our family has been through a lot," the young woman who Tessa had addressed said. "Ever since my sister Lynnie was kidnapped from our house when I was five, we've been split apart, everyone feeling their own grief and sadness and disappointment and guilt. Mostly guilt, because aren't parents supposed to take care of their child? Isn't a sister supposed to protect her little sister?"

Beth felt the breath whoosh out of her. She felt herself begin to tremble. She thought about years of counseling and trying to retrieve memories that hadn't been retrievable. She'd been three when her parents adopted her. She'd been abandoned at a mall. She'd either been too young to remember, or had traumatic amnesia. She figured her origins would always remain a secret.

But there was something about the woman who was speaking. They looked so much alike! And there was something about the older man and woman sitting there. There was something about the name *Lynnie.* There was something—

The longer Beth watched that TV screen, the longer something stirred inside of her. She wanted to reach out to this woman named Clare. She wanted to be with Amanda and Max Thaddeus...because that's where she felt she should be.

She remembered a house with green siding and black shutters. She remembered a huge yard. She remembered—Oh, Lord, she remembered.

Her breath coming in shallow pants now, she turned back to her computer, awakened it, searched for the cable news channel's website and found a phone number.

She picked up her phone and dialed.

Biography

Award-winning author Karen Rose Smith was born in Pennsylvania. Although she was an only child, she remembers the bonds of an extended family. Since her father came from a family of ten and her mother, a family of seven, there were always aunts, uncles and cousins visiting on weekends. Family is a strong theme in her books and she suspects her childhood memories are the reason.

In college, Karen began writing poetry and also met her husband to be. They both began married life as teachers, but when their son was born, Karen decided to try her hand at a home-decorating business. She returned to teaching for a while but changes in her life led her to writing romance fiction. Now she writes romances and mysteries full time.

Presently, she is hard at work on two mystery series—her Caprice De Luca Home Staging series as well as her Daisy's Tea Garden mysteries. When she isn't writing, she cares for her four rescued cats and assorted strays, cooks, gardens and photographs all. She enjoys interacting with her readers on social media.

Married to her college sweetheart since 1971, believing in the power of love and commitment, she envisions herself writing relationship novels, both romance and mystery, for a long time to come!

KAREN ROSE SMITH BOOKS
AVAILABLE IN E-BOOK FORMAT

FINDING MR. RIGHT Series
Kit and Kisses, Book 1*
Forever After, Book 2*
When Mom Meets Dad, Book 3 *
Falling For Her Boss, Book 4 *
Toys and Baby Wishes, Book 5 *
Love in Bloom, Book 6
Ribbons and Rainbows, Book 7 *
Wish on the Moon, Book 8 *
A Man Worth Loving, Book 9 *

SEARCH FOR LOVE Series
Nathan's Vow, Book 1 *
Jake's Bride, Book 2 *
Always Devoted, Book 3 *
Always Her Cowboy, Book 4 *
Heartfire, Book 5*
Cassidy's Cowboy, Book 6 *
Her Sister, Book 7 *

EVERYDAY LOVE Short Story Series
Everyday Cinderellas, Vol. 1
Everyday Prince Charming, Vol. 2
Everyday Romance, Vol.3

Garden of Fantasy
Abigail and Mistletoe
Writing is a Business

SCIENCE FICTION
SHORT STORY COLLECTION
Journey Into Chaos

BOXED SETS
Finding Mr. Right Box Set One
Finding Mr. Right Boxed Set Two
Search For Love Boxed Set One
Search For Love Boxed Set Two
Everyday Love Boxed Set

*Also available as an audio book

Excerpt from NATHAN'S VOW
Search For Love series, Book 1

Prologue

Don't answer it.
 Don't answer it.
*Do **not** answer it.*

Gillian Moore convinced herself to ignore the in-
trusive sound of the ringing telephone as the golden
L.A. sun swept through her open living room window,
along with the balmy June breeze.

Her phone rang a second time.

Plucking the leatherbound volumes from her book-
shelf one by one, she dusted them with a soft cloth. She
always cleaned and straightened her surroundings when
her heart or mind was in turmoil. With a quick glance
at the phone on her end table, she knew her mother
wouldn't be calling on a Monday evening. Madge
Moore called her daughter from Deep River, Indiana
every Sunday at exactly seven p.m.

Gillian's phone rang a third time.

She swiped the cloth across the shelf, back and

forth. In the three months since she'd relocated to L.A., she hadn't confided in anyone or encouraged close friendships. She needed this respite. She needed to find out whether her "gift" would continue to be the major force in her life or whether she had a right to keep it in the background, maybe even completely under wraps.

Her phone rang a fourth time.

It could only be **him**—the man who had called the past two nights, the man with the compelling voice, tinged with authority, commanding in its intensity as it directed her to return his call. She didn't know what he wanted, but she could guess. Heaven knew how he'd gotten her number because no one in L.A. had it, not even the manager where she worked.

Her answering machine kicked on with her brief direction for the caller to leave a message. Her usually lilting tone was serious and cool. She ran her hand through her long, light brown hair. Maybe she should get it cut short…make yet another change in her life. She'd made so many in moving here—she actually had time to herself...to be out in the sun, ride a bike, take long walks. She'd found peace along with the bright California sun and she wasn't ready to let go of either.

"Ms. Moore. This is Nathan Bradley. Again," he added in a deep, almost censuring baritone. "In case you haven't received my earlier messages, I need to speak with you immediately about a matter of great urgency." He paused. "Ms. Moore, I *must* speak with you. Please return my call." He gave his number slowly, hesitated a moment, then clicked off.

Gillian stopped dusting. He hadn't said "please" in

his other messages. This time there was a quiet desperation in his tone. She recognized the emotion because the people she'd helped in the past had all been desperate. Nathan Bradley didn't sound like a man who was accustomed to using the word "please," and the huskiness edging the word made her feel vulnerable and guilty, two of the burdens from which she'd tried to escape.

Now this man had brought them to the surface once more. She *wouldn't* return his call. She deserved unpressured time to think about the direction of her life, to have fun working at something she'd never imagined she'd enjoy. Nathan Bradley could find someone else to solve his problem, someone else with a "gift" that had begun to feel more like a curse.

Chapter One

Nathan didn't want to be caught dead, let alone alive, inside a beauty salon. As he pulled open the glass door and stepped inside, feminine chatter, strange smells, and the glimpse of a woman with her hair rolled in blue and purple curlers was enough to make him decide he'd rather face ten irate CEO's whose firewalls had been breached in one day than to plow into this women's domain. But he'd do anything to find his daughters.

Anything.

Nathan's determination had pulled him out of the poverty of his childhood, earned him a scholarship to college, and pushed him to start his own company specializing in computer security after only a year with another firm. He'd wanted to be his own boss, bill his own hours, set his own standards. His determination couldn't save his marriage, but by God, it would lead him to his daughters. After six months of dead ends, he'd decided money and rational strategies weren't enough. That's why he was here. That's why he had to speak to Gillian Moore.

At his private investigator's insistence, Nathan had agreed to go this route—the only route left as far as Nathan was concerned or he wouldn't pursue it. He wouldn't debate about methods, not even weird ones at this point. He'd used every skill he'd possessed to find his daughters. So had his P.I. Now he had to put his logic and wariness aside if he hoped to find his children before he lost more time with them.

The woman at the desk inside the door smiled as her gaze traveled from his dark brown hair, down his charcoal pinstripe suit and striped silk tie, to his black winged-tip shoes. She tilted her head and her lips curved up a bit more. "Can I help you?"

Suddenly Nathan felt as if he were the center of attention. Two customers on chairs in the room beyond had craned their necks to avidly assess him along with the receptionist. His shirt collar felt tighter, and he resisted the urge to tug down his tie. "I'm looking for Gillian Moore."

"You want a manicure?" the redheaded, perfectly coiffed and made-up receptionist asked with a mischievous smile.

"No. My name is Nathan Bradley. I need to speak with her as soon as possible," he said in his best authoritarian tone. "Is she here?"

"Hold on a sec," the redhead answered, her smile flagging. Disappearing into the room beyond, she reappeared a few moments later. "She's with a client. She says she'll talk to you in five minutes."

Five minutes. What the heck was he supposed to do for five minutes? He spied several magazines in a basket in the corner beside two director's chairs. "Fine. I'll wait."

Waiting wasn't something Nathan did well. He hadn't become a successful CEO with company locations across the country by waiting. As he flipped one glossy page after the other, he was vaguely aware this publication didn't advertise fast cars or designer clothes. Tuning in to the sound of feminine voices in the next room, he tried to pick out the one belonging to a woman who had helped police departments solve missing person cases. As he had many times in the past few days, he imagined what she might look like. Probably fuzzy, wild hair with a red scarf tied around her head.

He could feel the receptionist watching him as she pretended to study the schedule book. Finally, a customer with bright crimson nails emerged from the room beyond and gingerly opened her purse at the desk.

"Gillian can see you now," the desk-keeper informed him.

Gillian Moore's lack of response to his phone calls had irritated and frustrated Nathan. He was accustomed to being in charge. But his reason for being here brushed all that aside.

Striding into the busy room, he took it in with one glance—the chairs, mirrors, blow dryers, three hairdressers chatting to their customers. But then his gaze fell on the small white wrought-iron desk in the far corner and the woman sitting behind it. Her face turned away from him, she slid a pack of acrylic nails to the side of the glass top and straightened her manicure paraphernalia. At his approach, her gaze met his, and he almost stopped short.

She didn't look like a psychic.

Her long, light brown hair was laced with sunny blond highlights. A few tendrils wisped along her cheek. Her bangs wafted across her honey brows. But it was her huge brown eyes that almost immobilized him. They didn't appraise him physically...they looked into his soul. He didn't like the invasion.

Gillian had wished her client a good day and unnecessarily organized her work table, hoping Nathan Bradley had decided not to wait. When she turned her head and saw a tall man with resolve shouting from his furrowed dark brows, the set of his mouth, and his slightly squared jaw, she realized it would take more than a few unanswered phone messages to deter this man.

Taking a slow breath and maintaining eye contact, she slid her hands into the pockets of her white apron. Nathan Bradley wanted something from her, all right, and she couldn't give it. Not right now.

"Ms. Moore."

It was more statement than question. She nodded.

"Could we talk for a few minutes?"

She gestured to her desk. "I'm working, Mr. Bradley. I really don't have time—"

"You don't have a client at the moment," he countered, his blue eyes steady, his voice firm.

This man could be intimidating. But she was used to dealing with hard-nosed cops, jaded private investigators, and a disbelieving public who wanted her help anyway. "No, I don't. But I am working. Now, if you'd like a manicure..." She almost had to smile at his expression of distaste, but then his next words made her heart beat faster.

"I want a few minutes with you. You're the last option I have."

"For what?" she asked, though she sensed what he needed.

"My two daughters. I need you to help me find them."

As she stood, Gillian glanced around the shop to make sure no one was listening. "Where did you get my name?"

"Does it matter?" As he asked, he slipped a photo from the inside pocket of his jacket.

His movement was quick, but Gillian caught a view of a narrow waist, slim hips, and a physique probably as taut as his demeanor and voice. When he offered her the photograph, her attention returned to the situation at hand and she took a step back.

The two young girls in the snapshot had their father's blue eyes and brown hair. She could tell that he loved them from the way the camera had caught Nathan Bradley' expression as he crouched down between them, one arm around each daughter. The pain in his eyes now attested to the fact.

He tried to hand Gillian the photo, but she wouldn't take it. She knew what might happen if she did. She might see images and feel emotions she didn't want right now. Folding her hands in front of her, she said, "I'm no longer doing that type of work."

But it was difficult for her to tear her gaze from the picture. When she did, the sadness in Nathan Bradley's eyes was almost as difficult to ignore.

"Why?"

For some reason, she couldn't hedge or lie to this man. Checking again to be sure no one eavesdropped, Gillian lowered her voice anyway. "Since I was sixteen, Mr. Bradley, my life hasn't been my own. I came to L.A. to escape the type of work you want me to do and to make decisions about my future." She stopped and tears pricked her eyes as she thought about the last few months before leaving Indiana.

Regaining her composure, she swallowed and went on, "For almost ten years, I've helped others when they've asked. Now I need time and breathing room before I decide if and how I want to use my gift again."

As she spoke, she could tell he listened. There was a spark of empathy in his eyes, but, of course, his need was more important. "Take this one case," he insisted. "I'll protect your privacy if that's what you're concerned about. Your help doesn't have to be public knowledge. I'm an internet security specialist. I know what safeguards we can take. No one else has to know you're here."

She steeled herself against the man's masculine appeal and turned away from the wonderful smiles of the children in the photo as well as the hurt still lingering in her heart. That hurt sprang up every time she remembered Brian Reston and the search for his son, the months she'd dreamed about a future for the three of them.

Despite the time that had passed, despite the miles between L.A. and Deep River, Indiana, she knew she wasn't ready for Nathan Bradley and his search...for any of it. The general public thought psychics could "know" anything they wanted, that they could answer any question, even their own personal ones. That just wasn't true. Gillian had realized early on that she couldn't use her "gift" for her own benefit or to predict events. All she could do was tune into impressions and use them along with her intuition. Words, pictures, and sounds sometimes popped into her head, but she never knew when that was going to happen. It hadn't happened since she'd left Indiana.

With the need for self-preservation being her overriding concern, she said, "If you found me, others will be able to. And I'm not only concerned about privacy. You make my help seem simple, as if all I have to do is close my eyes and give you the answers you want. The process is much more complicated than that. Try a private investigator, Mr. Bradley. It will be best for both of us."

"A private investigator gave me your name."

She sighed and shook her head. "Then he can find someone else who does my kind of work."

"It's difficult to find a reputable psychic," Nathan almost growled as his frustration became evident.

Worry stabbed Gillian. "Sh..." All she needed was her co-workers knowing.

Nathan lifted his hands in exasperation and in a loud whisper asked, "Why is it so all-fired important for no one to know what you do?"

Anger bubbled up inside her because this man

knew nothing about the hundreds of letters she received each year, the sleepless nights, the burden of parents and brothers and sisters and children depending on her to find someone they loved, or someone who was missing. What irritated her the most were those who wanted a plan for the future without formulating it themselves. "If they knew what I was able to do, most women in this salon would want a reading. They'd line up for hours waiting with bated breath for me to tell them their future. And if I couldn't tell them anything, they'd say I'm a fraud. My gift creates a three-ring circus, Mr. Bradley. No, thank you."

Harriet came in from the front desk. "A walk-in for nails is waiting, Gillian. How's your schedule?"

Gillian accepted fate's offer of a neat, non-confrontational way to end this encounter. "Tell her to come in. I don't have another appointment until four. If it's all right with you, I'll take my supper break at five."

"No problem." Harriet's interest in Nathan was obvious as she gave him a wink and returned to the front room.

He faced Gillian. "I'd like to continue our discussion."

"There's nothing more to say. I have to get back to work and I'm sure you do, too. Call your P.I. He'll find someone else."

The look the man gave Gillian was not resigned. If anything, it was more determined than ever. But he didn't argue. "I'll call my P.I. But I'll be talking to you again. Soon."

With a lift of his brow and a wave of his hand, he was gone.

Gillian first felt relief, then a strange sense of loss. But she was used to feelings and images not clicking. Eventually they became part of a bigger picture, and then she'd understand. But there was no bigger picture where Nathan Bradley was concerned. There was no picture at all.

The instant Gillian stepped outside of the Hair Happening, she saw him. He stood beside a gray Mercedes in the parking lot. She should have realized this man wouldn't give up so easily. Ducking back into the salon was an option. So was ignoring him as she walked to the enchilada and chili stand across the parking lot of the strip shopping center. But she had the feeling when she returned, he'd still be waiting, and not quite so patiently.

A group of teenagers on roller-blades skated by, one of them holding a miniature schnauzer on a leash. She smiled at the sight, something she'd probably never see in Deep River. But her smile slipped as she spotted the handsome, very sexy man walking toward her, and an excited little shiver zipped up her spine. At least six-two, lean and fit, with long legs that quickly covered the distance between them, he was the type of man who could attract a roomful of women without trying. It wasn't only his looks but his confidence, his dominating male presence.

When he stood before her, he asked, "Can I buy you supper?"

"If I hadn't mentioned my break, you would have waited till I quit for the day. Right?"

"Yes."

"Mr. Bradley..."

"Nathan. You have to eat supper. I have to eat supper. Is there any reason we shouldn't talk while we do?"

"You have an ulterior motive. This won't be much of a break for me."

"It's not an ulterior motive because you know what I want."

"Obviously, I need to watch what I say with you," she murmured.

The corners of his mouth twitched up. "Is that a yes or no?"

"If I say no, you'll be back. Let's get this over with."

The curve of his lips turned into a frown, indicating he was uncomfortable with her frankness. Gillian's gaze wanted to linger on those lips. They were full enough to be sensual, narrow enough to enhance the handsome aesthetics of his face. She could imagine one of his kisses—dominating, forceful, passion-filled.

The image startled her. She hadn't thought about kissing a man in over a year—since Brian had decided to reconcile with his ex-wife. She'd not only lost Brian but his son, too. At the time she'd thought her heart would break. But she'd buried herself in her work until she'd realized she no longer had a life outside of her work. Not eating, not sleeping, working twenty hours a day was a one-way road to disaster. Thank goodness she'd recognized her destructive direction in time.

"I don't know what you have in mind," she said,

"but the chili and enchiladas are good at that stand over there."

Nathan perused the truck/restaurant set-up near an island with palm trees and benches. "I haven't had an enchilada in..." He shrugged. "Too long."

They walked side by side for a few moments, Nathan slowing his stride to Gillian's. The breeze ruffled his hair, making him look less formal and imposing. She thought he'd start making his case for her help, but he didn't.

His arm brushed hers, his suitcoat rough against her skin. "Have you always done manicures for a living?"

She registered the texture of the material, the strength of his arm, and her heart jumped at the contact. Managing a smile, she responded, "Would you believe I have a degree in business?"

"Neither seems appropriate for a psychic."

Her smile faded. "And what does? Theater arts?"

He stopped and faced her. "Okay. I stuck my foot in it. I didn't mean to insult you. But all this is strange to me. I'm a logical man. I make decisions and judgments from facts. I've always thought psychics were frauds. But my private investigator told me about crimes you've solved and people you've found. Even if I don't believe in it or understand it, what you do works."

"I don't understand it, either," she said quietly.

Nathan had been fascinated by the woman since he'd set his eyes on her. Looking at her now, her soft, long hair, those wonderful brown eyes, her slender curves wrapped in a pink cullotte dress with a white collar and lapels, his muscles tightened and he felt pangs of arousal.

Crazy. That usually didn't happen simply from looking.

Her soft voice, her calm wonder, urged him to step closer, to find out more about her. "Tell me about it. Were you born with this ability?"

She shook her head and pointed to the supper truck. They began walking again. "I don't think I was born with it. If I was, I didn't know it until I was ten. I was sitting on a dock fishing and a storm came up. The thunder and lightning hit fast. The next thing I knew I was lying flat on the dock, the rain pouring down on me. My head hurt and I was shaking all over. Mom found me that way, took me home, and put me to bed. We thought that was the end of it."

His P.I. had told Nathan that Gillian was from Indiana and had lived there all her life. She traveled often but had never moved from the town where she'd grown up. L.A. must be quite a change for her. "When did you realize something was different?"

"A few days later. Aunt Flora came to visit. When she hugged me, I saw this picture of her sitting at her kitchen table crying. I didn't understand it. Later, I overheard my aunt and my mother talking. My cousin had dropped out of high school and my aunt was terribly upset."

"And there was no way you could have known that."

"No."

"Did you tell your mom?"

"No. I was afraid of the pictures when they came and uncomfortable with the feelings. I kept it a secret until I was sixteen."

They reached the vending stand. Gillian ordered chili and cornbread while Nathan asked for an enchilada. She opened her purse, but he closed his hand over hers. Her skin was soft and warm and a jolt of desire more powerful than before stabbed him. "I've got it," he said, unable to keep the husky rasp from his voice.

Her gaze met his. The sparks of gold in the brown told him his touch affected her as much as hers affected him. She pulled away, and he let go.

Gillian busied herself pulling napkins from the holder while Nathan paid for and carried their plates to a bench. Picking up their sodas, she joined him. She'd no sooner settled on the bench with her soda by her shoe and the cup of chili with a wedge of cornbread perched on the edge in her hand when the schnauzer she'd seen earlier ran over to her and jumped up and down, finally landing with her paws on Gillian's knees.

Gillian laughed and held her dish a little higher, out of the dog's reach. "You might want supper, but I'm not sure you should have this."

One of the roller-bladers came skating over, his helmet under his arm, a leash dangling from his hand. "Sorry if she's botherin' you. She begs from everybody."

The boy was about twelve. His spiked brown hair was matted down from his helmet, his snapping brown eyes sparkled with amusement. Gillian asked him, "Can she have a bite?"

He grinned. "If you wanna give it to her."

Gillian tried to tear off a piece of the cornbread, but it slid into the chili. Nathan grabbed the dish and held it for her. Smiling her thanks, she took the small bite from the wedge and let the dog lick it from her hand. The schnauzer gulped it down and looked up at her for more. Laughing again, Gillian scratched the pet behind her ears. "I should have known that little bit wouldn't be enough."

As she touched the dog and rubbed her rough coat, Gillian felt her gaze pulled to the teenager again. He and the dog were connected by a strong bond of affection. A surge of energy made her fingers tingle and she automatically closed her eyes for a moment. A clear picture of a dark-haired woman on a porch came into focus. The woman was worried. Gillian had the distinct impression she was the boy's mother.

Opening her eyes, Gillian cast a wary look at Nathan. He was watching her closely. Should she say something to the boy about his mother? If she did, Nathan would know what had happened. Why had this vision come now? Since she'd left Indiana, she'd felt normal—no pictures, no knowledge she shouldn't have.

Gillian looked at the boy, knowing she couldn't let the woman in her mind's eye suffer unnecessarily. "I think your dog wants a full-course meal."

"What time is it?" he asked with a nod at Gillian's watch.

"Five-thirty."

"Geez. I was supposed to be home an hour ago. Mom's gonna be..." He stopped with a shrug as if a boy his age shouldn't worry about adult authority. Snapping the leash onto the dog's collar, he gave it a gentle tug. "C'mon, Peanut. We'll get us both some supper." He smiled at Gillian and skated over to his friends, who sat on the curb sipping sodas.

Nathan handed Gillian her plate. "What happened?"

"You saw what happened. I gave the dog a snack."

"When you touched the dog, you closed your eyes."

The man was too observant. "The boy's mother was worried about him."

"You felt that?"

"I saw that. She was standing on the porch waiting for him."

"You got that from petting the dog?" Nathan asked, astonished.

She'd faced expressions like his many times in the past. "Mr. Bradley..."

"Nathan," he reminded her.

Calling him by his first name seemed too familiar. She already knew she could be attracted to him. "This 'talent' I have isn't something I can turn off and on like a light switch. It's more unpredictable than the weather or earthquakes."

"You made him realize she was worried without saying it, without telling him you knew."

"That was easiest."

Nathan finished his enchilada and took a swig of soda before he spoke again. "My ex-wife took my daughters out of the country six months ago. I can't find them. My P.I. can't find them. Will you take my case?"